A LOVE STORY

A LOVE STORY

Enrique Muchacho

Apprentice House Press

Loyola University Maryland

First Edition

Hardcover ISBN: 978-1-62720-366-1
Paperback ISBN: 978-1-62720-367-8
Ebook ISBN: 978-1-62720-368-5

Printed in the United States of America

Published by Apprentice House Press

Apprentice
House Press
Loyola University Maryland

Loyola University Maryland
4501 N. Charles Street
Baltimore, MD 21210
410.617.5265
www.ApprenticeHouse.com • info@ApprenticeHouse.com

For those looking to dream and/or escape.

1

What I pray for during every Sunday sermon is for the service to go faster. So, when the priest ends it by telling us to go in peace, I quietly mutter a "thank God" under my breath and start moving.

I get up from my seat and head towards the exit. The rest of the crowd does the same. Family members get together and make their way from their seats to the front door. Some of them occasionally stop to say goodbye to someone and maybe end up talking. The priest has already left the stand, but as usual, he'll be out in the front waiting for the crowd to come out. He'll stand there, do the occasional handshake with those walking by, pass a few words to those who thank him or ask for guidance, and, once everyone leaves, he'll do whatever it is that priests do when the sermon ends–probably get the place ready for the next one.

Halfway to the exit, I slow my pace. Knowing my dad, he won't be happy that I bolted from my seat without saying goodbye to anyone. He'll most likely give me a lecture about loving my neighbor, along with an accusation that I should know better. I also know that we'll be here an extra ten or twenty minutes which he'll spend saying goodbye to other parents while jumping into a conversation. I sigh. I'd complain to him, but like the times before, it's not going to get me anywhere. Might as well just let him do his thing and head outside to take a breather.

I don't exactly hate going to church. I used to love coming here with my parents every Sunday when I was younger. But I was only a kid. Now, I'm seventeen and they should already know that I've changed. Time went by and I no longer see the point of going to church every Sunday. It's not like if I miss one sermon, I'll be on a front row seat on my way to hell. Some people don't go to church unless it's a special occasion like Christmas or Lent, but my dad sure isn't going to let me slide off on missing a service at all, especially after last night.

The memory of all that happened comes flowing back: how I told them I needed to say something, how

I told them, how mom's expression changed, and how dad threw a fit and slapped me so hard that it left a mark on my left cheek. I could tell that he wanted to do more than that. It was written in his eyes, but he held it back for the sole reason we had church in the morning. People would notice. He's lucky that the handprint was gone by then. If I showed up with even the slightest sign that I was slapped, people would talk, and my dad is not in the mood to be burdened any more than he already is.

Honestly, I don't get it. I can break a couple of biblical rules because they find it's okay, but when I say that I'm into boys instead of girls, they start ranting on about how it's a sin and that I'll burn in hell for it. I wanted to argue with them, and I had a semi-good argument that might move things in my favor, but their reactions struck me harder than I thought they would. I thought that coming out was supposed to be this beautiful moment where they would show me their love and support and tell me that everything's going to be alright. Instead, I got the opposite and a smack from my dad–my welcoming sign to my new reality along with the possibility of who knows what other problems might arrive. After slapping me, he told me to go to my room, and that's where I stayed until the morning. One of my parents—my mom, I think—peeked through the door to check on me. I brought my sobbing to a halt until they left.

I didn't sleep much that night. So many thoughts flew through my head that I didn't doze off until a few hours before dawn. When they woke me up for church, I asked if I could skip it for one day, but dad responded with a no right away. There was anger and disappointment in his voice. He's probably thinking that I fell out of line with God and that if I find my way back, I'll stop liking guys. I wasn't in the mood to complain or argue, so I just got up from bed and readied myself for the sermon.

The hardest part was what came next. During breakfast, the drive to church, and the sermon, they looked uncomfortable around me, as if I were a stranger to them. Maybe that's exactly what I am. I'm not the son they always thought I was. I kept a side of me hidden from them and now that it's out in the open, things are different between us. I wonder if they think that they failed as parents and that's why I'm gay, or maybe that it's my own fault. It doesn't matter anyway.

Wondering what they think won't change that they

don't accept me, and that they don't want anyone to know. My dad will make sure to keep me quiet. He's most likely planning on keeping me on a leash so tight that he'll be breathing down my neck during every decision of my day-to-day life. I'll keep my head down and do what he says. Seems to be the only thing I can do for now. I'm still not giving up. I'll find a way to reason with them.

I just need to find out how.

When I walk out through the doors, I take in the fresh air and little taste of freedom for as long as I can. As soon as mom and dad finish with their goodbyes, we'll head back home, which is not worrying me so much since they won't speak about it, but they'll still do something. My thoughts focus on what they might do. Maybe they'll just ship me off to some conversion clinic. That's what Mr. and Mrs. Bartow did with their son, so who's to say that my parents won't do the same thing?

Everyone remembers how it happened: Mr. and Mrs. Bartow sent Kyle away with no explanation except that he was going to "find his way back." They never said anything about conversion therapy, but it was written between the lines. After that day, no one has seen

Kyle for six months and his parents don't talk much about how he's doing. God only knows what they're doing to him—pills, electroshock therapy, torture. A shiver runs through my spine at the thought.

Think positive Taylor, I tell myself. *Think positive.*

I try distracting myself with the scene around me. People of all ages walk around the entrance talking with their neighbors and friends. Parents say goodbye to other parents or stay together and have small discussions. Children talk and laugh a bit or try to maneuver their parents to take them home. The priest stands in the center of it all, doing everything I knew he'd be doing. I watch the crowds of people go over to him, telling him to have a good day, asking for guidance, or just saying goodbye.

Eventually, my eyes fall on a boy my age who's sitting on the steps with his back resting on a column. His blonde hair is wrapped up in dozens of curls with a few of them covering a portion of his forehead. His eyes are relaxed, but focused in some way, and man are they blue. If I look right, I can see how they seem to sparkle with the sunlight. A tiny scar runs diagonally through his right eyebrow. He's dressed in his Sunday best, which in this case consists of a nice pair of tennis shoes, some jeans, and a white polo shirt. I smile.

He's beautiful.

"Marcus," I hear my dad's voice call out.

For a second, I think that's the boy's name, but then my dad passes me and shakes the hand of a man I don't recognize. His black hair is neatly combed back with what I think might be too much gel. His dark blue eyes are hidden behind a pair of glasses. He's dressed in a black suit with a white-collar shirt. When my dad approaches him, they shake hands, after which I'm thrown into the conversation when my dad says, "And this is my son Taylor."

Marcus turns to me. "Nice to meet you Taylor," he tells me. I shake his hand. His grip is strong, but also a bit loose. I eye my dad for a second. A smile rests on his face. It's probably fake. He was still mad at me when I woke up and I doubt that one church service will make him forget.

Marcus lets go of my hand, then he goes back to talking to my dad. I go back to looking for that guy. I find him again standing next to a woman, who might be his mother. They have a few similarities, like their hair and eyes. Their faces, however, look different. His facial muscles seem more relaxed than his mother's. I smile again. He really is cute.

A moment comes that he turns to face me, and I immediately tune into the conversation while silently praying that he didn't take notice of how I was staring at him. I manage to catch a few details from them. Apparently, Marcus is the new pastor for the church. It seems that the father is retiring so he's going to be taking charge here starting tomorrow. He and his family just got here on Friday. "You know," Marcus says to me, "I have a son about your age. Maybe you two could hang out sometime and you could show him around."

I turn to look at dad. He's still smiling, but I can read the worry within his eyes. I fight not to roll mine. I want to tell him that just because I'm gay doesn't mean that I'm going to fall for every boy that comes my way. Even still, he'll be cautious, just like when he still thought that I liked girls. I turn to Marcus and say, "That'd be nice. Where's he at?"

Marcus scans the crowd. "He's... umm... over there. Matthew!"

I turn around and my heart climbs up my throat. It's him. He's walking towards us, slowly and simply, obediently at the command of his father. When he gets here, Marcus says, "Taylor, this my son Matthew. Matthew, this is Taylor."

"It's nice to meet you," he says.

We shake hands, and a moment of panic comes through me. *I'm shaking his hand!* It's warm. My heartbeat accelerates. I try my best not to look panicked. Once our handshake comes to an end, Marcus looks at Matthew and says, "I was just talking about how maybe Taylor could show you around town sometime."

Matthew looks at me. His blue eyes study my face as if he were trying to read through me. I keep calm. I don't smile, I don't widen my eyes or do anything that would give out a sign that I'm freaking out a bit, especially with my dad here. If he takes notice of this, he'll be keeping me as far away from him as he can. Finally, Matthew speaks. "That'd be nice, if that's okay with you."

I raise my shoulders. "Sure. Why not?"

"Then it's settled," Marcus says, "You two can hang out tonight."

"Tonight," I say, trying my best to not sound shocked.

"Yes, tonight. Your father was kind enough to invite us over for dinner. We have no plans, and the kitchen is still not set up, so we accepted."

I turn to Matthew. He looks at me for a second and smiles—a beautiful smile—then turns to look at his father. Our dad's keep on talking, and Matthew listens to the conversation. Immediately, I stop looking at Matthew and try to focus on the discussion, but despite listening to their voices, I get lost in my own thoughts. All of them are about Matthew.

So, not only do I crush on a guy I just happen to meet outside of church, but now I find out that he's the son of the new pastor, and he's coming over to my house for dinner. If that's not the world messing with me, I don't know what is. I think of Matthew. He is cute, and I definitely like him, but he doesn't strike me as gay. Then again, my parents didn't think I was gay until I told them last night. Maybe I'm right and he isn't gay. Or maybe I'm wrong.

I think about the way he was staring at me. He looked at me as if he were trying to read me. Maybe he was trying to read *through* me. Maybe he wanted to know if I was hiding something, or he noticed that I was watching him and now he's curious as to why I was doing that. Or maybe that was his way of getting to know people. Not everyone gets to know someone the same way.

Or maybe—and this is a big maybe—he was looking for a sign. Maybe he was looking for any sort of hint that would give him an answer to his search. Maybe he was looking for what I'm praying to find in him.

Maybe he's looking to see if I am what I am.

2

A thirty-minute car ride later, we were back home. Once inside, I head to my room and change into something more comfortable.

I lie on my bed and stare at the ceiling. It's the only thing I can do to pass the time in here. If I wanted to, I could go out and meet up with my friends, but with my relationship with my parents being on thin ice, it is probably best if I stay in here until things cool off. Even if things do cool off, they'll still put in their restrictions, like with whom I can hang out with, when we hang out, how long I can be there and where I can go. It's all going to be dads' choice; mom won't have a say in this.

Now that I think of it, my mom rarely stands up for what she believes. She barely raises her voice to give out an opinion, and when it came to me coming out, she didn't say a word. I'm not even sure if she's okay with me being gay or not. I haven't asked her about it, and she hasn't brought it up. I did hear some arguing last night after I went upstairs, but what it was about, I don't know. Maybe mom was going against dad. If so, it wouldn't be the first time.

For the past two or three years, I feel like my parents have been putting up an act just for me. Even before last night, I would sometimes hear some commotion from downstairs or from their bedroom and when I'd come in to see what was going on, they would stop arguing and say that it's just "grown-up problems." At first, I thought it was just that, but lately the arguments have become more of a routine. There were times that they would fight through screams or discussions. Other times they would just exchange mean looks. When it was the latter, they waited for me to be out of the room before they started arguing.

I shake those thoughts out of my head, but they keep crawling back in. I need a serious distraction. I pull my phone out and open a text chain with Nora.

> **Me:** Hey. Think you can talk?
> A minute passes before she replies.
> **Nora:** Sure. What's up?"

Me: I told them last night. Didn't go well.
   <<sad emoji>>
Nora: Ouch. Care to talk about it?

I set the phone down. My dad doesn't want anyone to know, but Nora's known about this for a while now. To be honest, she found out the same time I acknowledged it: seven minutes in heaven in Kylie Monroe's closet. We went in when it was our turn and none of it was fun or exciting for me. By then, I was questioning what I liked and possibly denying the truth, but that time in the closet was all it took for me to face it once and for all.

When we came out, she confronted me about it. We talked in private and after I came out to her, she gave me a hug and told me that she would be there for me and that was that.

The next person I told was our friend Alex. He was cool about it, as well; he even helped me out in coming to terms with it. There weren't many kids I could talk to. Most of them are not out of the closet–or they are, and have it either good or bad at home and school because of it. When I was going through some bad thoughts, he and Nora would cheer me up in the best ways they could think of, which in one case involved me chowing down on a giant sundae until I got a brain freeze. They also helped me do research and offered me pieces of advice, one of which was for me not to come out to my parents because they thought that they wouldn't accept me. We were in the Mid-Atlantic part of the country, so I could understand their concerns, but I still thought that my parents wouldn't care about it.

I guess I should've listened to them.

> **Me:** Not much to say. I told them I was gay, then my dad slapped me in the face.
> **Nora:** WTF?!?! He slapped you!
> **Me:** Yup
> **Nora:** Really?! What an ass.
> **Me:** <<sigh emoji>> Yup. That's my dad. A total ass.
> **Nora:** Yikes! Are u ok? How u feelin?
> **Me:** How does one feel when they're rejected? <<worried emoji>>
> **Nora:** Can I come over?

I think of dad. He'll turn her away with some excuse and I can't risk him getting suspicious.

> **Me:** Probably best if you don't. Things are still heated up and bringing you might bring problems.
> **Nora:** Your parents really have problems.
> **Me:** Well, it's mainly my dad, but yeah. They

do have problems.
Nora: Well, anything else happen?

I set the phone down. Is this the point where I tell her about my crush on the new pastor's son? Nora's good at keeping secrets and she's been pretty quiet about my secret. I guess I can open up about it.

> **Me:** Did you hear that there's a new pastor in the church?
> **Nora:** Yeah. My mom told me about it. His family just moved here from the west.
> **Me:** Well, he and his family are coming over for dinner tonite.
> **Nora:** Any kids your age?
> **Me:** Their son, Matthew.
> **Nora:** Care to describe him?

My first thought is to send her a "no", but that would just make me look suspicious so, I go with something simple.

> **Me:** Blonde, blue eyed, kind of fit, dresses nice also.
> **Nora:** OMG!!! You're totally crushing on him.

I sigh. I should've probably gone with a "no" instead.

Me: <<middle finger emoji>> Am not.
Nora: Yes, you are. I know you so well.
   <<smirk emoji>>
Me: <<eye roll emoji>> Ok. Maybe I am, but
   still…
Nora: What? It's ok if you have a little crush.
   Doesn't mean much.
Me: It does if he's the pastor's son. You think
   my parents are bad? His could be worse.
Nora: So he's gay too?
Me: Not sure. I'll find out, but in time.
Nora: Kay.

At that point, my bedroom door opens up a bit and my mom creeps through the opening. She's still dressed in her Sunday best, but she's switched out her footwear for something a little more comfortable. I straighten myself on my bed.

"Is something wrong?" I ask.

She shakes her head. "I just wanted to tell you that your father went out to run some errands. He'll be back in an hour."

"Okay," I say.

My phone dings. It's another message from Nora. Panic flows through me. If they find out that she knows the truth, who knows what'll happen. "Who are you texting?" my mom asks.

I keep calm and reply. "Nora."

My mom walks into my room and shuts the door behind her. My heartbeat accelerates. "What are you talking about?"

I want to answer her with what business is that of hers, but I'm already on thin ice with her and dad. "Just some stuff," I say.

"*Some stuff*," my mom says questionably.

I keep my cool. My heartbeat is already on the rise. My palms are filling with sweat. My breathing is calm, but she'll take notice of the rest sooner or later. "We were just talking about making plans to hang out some time," I lie. It wasn't a total lie. We did talk about making plans to hang out this week, only it wasn't today.

My mother doesn't say anything. Instead, she walks over to me and sits beside me. Her presence frightens me more. She's not like dad. She didn't hit me, scream at me, or show any signs of anger when I came out. She did look shocked, but she never got a chance to tell me her thoughts, so I have no idea what she's thinking.

She could be bottling up her anger, keeping it buried so she doesn't react like dad did. She could be denying it. If she is, she's probably telling herself that it's all just a phase or something and that it'll go away. Maybe she's disappointed, either in me or herself. Either way, it would hurt me the same.

I try to hold back the tears. To be honest, I don't want to have to hold the pain back. I want to cry and scream and roll into a ball and try to find comfort in doing so. I feel like leaving, packing up a bag, and taking off. Maybe I could go to Nora's. Her family seems like they would accept me. But I don't want to leave. I want to stay with my parents and convince them that I'm alright, but I don't even know how to start doing that.

"Taylor," my mom says gently, placing a hand on my shoulder. Her touch frightens me for a second before I begin to calm down. There was something familiar about that touch. It felt the same way when Nora hugged me after I told her I was gay. *Is this a sign?* I ask myself. Is this her way of telling me that she loves me? If so, I need a clearer message.

At that moment, my mom lifts her arms up and wraps me in an embrace. She drags my upper body down to her stomach and I feel her body heat pass on to my head. She gently soothes my back and runs a hand through my hair. That always calms me down. She leans into my head and whispers "I love you," into my ear before letting me go and walking out of my room.

For a moment, I'm surprised. She just said that she loves me but didn't say anything else. She didn't even come back to check on me anytime soon. Was it to calm me down or because she means it? Sometimes, I don't think she means what she says, but she sounded like she meant it.

Maybe this is her way of breaking free from dad. Maybe this is how she plans to resist him. She'll do it by accepting me.

And she's just taken the first step.

3

The rest of the day goes by fast and thankfully, not a single argument occurs. As the sun sets, I go clean up before Matthew's family arrives.

I hit the shower and scrub my thin body as hard as I can. Then, I dig a fresh shirt and some jeans out of my closet and put them on. I comb my brown hair as neatly as possible, before proceeding to brush my teeth so hard that all I can taste is mint. Before heading down, I take one last look in the mirror. I look nice, maybe too nice. I mess my hair up a little in hopes that it looks like I'm not dressed to impress. It works well.

I'll be honest, I'm still not satisfied with how I look. I want to gain some muscle, get a haircut, clear my face of a few pimples, and maybe, just maybe see if I could stretch an inch or two until I'm about the same height as Matthew. Still, I can't. I don't have the time, and Matthew would notice the changes. I'll have to work with what I have.

By the time I come down, both my parents had changed clothes as well. My mom went with something casual, so she put on a blouse with a pair of jeans. Dad, on the other hand, dressed up a little too nice for a dinner at home, but I keep my mouth shut.

To be honest, I don't get why dad invited them over so soon. I know they just moved here, but if I were him, I would've given them a few days to settle in before doing so. But a part of me is glad that he did because it means I get to see Matthew again. Since we left church, I've been longing for the next time we'd be in the same place together. I want to talk to him, look at him, be next to him. I want to see him smile, hear him laugh, feel his touch. *His touch*: thinking about when we shook hands runs a chill through my spine.

In my head, I pray that he's gay. Even if he isn't, I feel like I can relate to him. We both have parents who are extremely devoted to their beliefs, and in turn, try to pass the rules down to us. I felt it when I stared into his eyes. Apart from him looking for something inside of me, in a way he seemed... trapped. He looked like he was stuck somewhere and dreaming of an escape. Something was burning within him, and it would burn brighter if he were free.

Maybe I'm getting this wrong. Maybe I'm just describing him based on my expectations. Maybe I'm describing myself and what I'm longing for. I'm not sure. Please God, let him be as good as I imagine, if not more.

The doorbell rings and I get to my feet. "I'll get it," I yell out. I open the door and there he is.

He's combed his hair a little bit, but his curls are fighting to go back to their regular form. The light from the ceiling brightens up his blue irises. He's dressed in a pair of blue jeans along with a nice pair of sneakers, but the white-collar shirt with the sleeves rolled up a bit makes him look nicer. In his hands is a bottle of wine, an offering from his parents to mine. I look at him and smile.

I feel the insatiable urge to kiss him. I imagine that I do. The second my lips touch his, he kisses me back and pulls me closer to him. Our chests converge, mixing the warmth of our lips and chests. After that, we separate, smiling at each other. He tells me he loves me. I do the same and no matter who stares at us, we make it worth their time.

But none of that happens. Instead, I say, "Hi," so hyper that it was probably a dead giveaway that I'm excited to see him.

"Hello," he replies. "Taylor, right?"

I hold back my excitement. He remembers my name. "Yeah," I say normally. I point to the bottle. "Is that for my parents?"

Matthew nods. "My parents wanted to thank them for inviting them for dinner so… they hope they like red."

"Well, they're more into whites, but they'll drink it either way."

"Cool," Matthew says. I take in how he said it. So quick, yet so… soulful. It felt like a blessing to hear it. I smile.

Matthew raises an eyebrow, but before he could ask why I smiled or anything, his parents come up from behind him. His mother is dressed in a pair of white jeans with a black blouse. Her hair is tucked back into a low ponytail. Marcus is dressed in a collar shirt with some jeans and a pair of dress shoes. His hair is neatly combed just like when I first saw him. As they stand in front of me, I think to myself, *They look like the perfect family.*

"Sorry we're late," Marcus says. "We got lost on the drive here. Is your father here?"

"Yes," my dad says as he appears from behind me. He shakes Marcus' hand and says, "Welcome. Dinner's not ready yet, so there's still some time to talk."

"That sounds nice," Matthew's mom says. "Matthew, why don't you go upstairs to hang out with Taylor?"

I can feel that my dad's expression had changed. "Why don't we all go into the living room instead? We could open that bottle of wine."

"That sounds great," Marcus replies, "but Matthew rarely finds an interest in grownup discussions. Maybe we should let the boys hang on their own."

"I'm not sure," my dad says. "We could find something interesting to tal—"

"Do you want to head up to my room or not?" I say breaking in.

My dad eyes me with a patronizing gaze and I think how I might as well have told him that I like him. Stupid. Stupid. *Stupid!* I want to scream or slap myself, anything to punish myself. But I can't do it now. I'm going to have to deal with whatever happens next.

Obviously, I'll first have to deal with my dad.

There's no way he would ever allow us to be up in my room all alone. He'll probably think that I'll try something. I've seen it before, the way he looks at me when I get a little too friendly with other boys. He was worried that it would mean that I was gay. Maybe he knew before I told him, and maybe he was denying it. I guess when I came out, he had to face the truth.

Then there's Matthew. Going upstairs to my room won't seem like anything weird to him. We could chat or maybe just play some videogames, if he wants to. I'm more worried about me. He makes me nervous, but that's only because I like him. And it's that nervousness that scares me into being in a room with him. If he isn't gay and I make a move, I'm dead. He'll tell his parents, who will tell my parents, and then I'll be in serious hot water.

"If that's okay with you, it's okay with me," Matthew says.

I'm both happy and frightened by his answer, but I make sure not to show either emotion. I turn to my dad and stare at his face. He's worried, and there's no doubt about it. He'll probably give me a warning either before I head up with him, or after he and his family leave. He'll probably stay down here wondering what we're doing up there, or mainly what I'm doing. "Okay then," I say. "Come on in."

Matthew nods and he and his family waltz inside. Matthew's parents head for the living room where they sit down and start talking with my mom. Matthew and I head upstairs, but we had to pass my dad to do so. He watched us—mainly me—go as we went up. His face seems to be saying, *Whatever you're thinking about doing, don't.* I want to roll my eyes, tell him to calm down, ask him why he thinks that I'm going to try something on every boy I hang out with. Instead, I just nod as I pass him by and head up the stairs.

Matthew follows right behind me. For a brief second, he's close enough that I can feel his body heat from behind. His breath hits me. The hairs on my back rise. Goosebumps run through me.

I think about the little details about him. The way his eyes stare at me, how they brighten up with the light, how his hair looks under the sunlight. I feel like my insides are melting. He's so damn hot, and I'd give anything to kiss him right now. I keep my head down and avoid turning to him. I don't want to give any hints about my feelings for him.

My body doesn't cooperate. It happens again—the

closeness, the heat, the breath—and this time, a strong chill runs through me that makes me shake a little.

Matthew takes notice. "Are you okay?" he asks me.

I look back at him. "I'm just cold," I say and keep on walking.

I can't recall what happens when we get to my room. All I know is that when we come in, he sits down in my desk chair while I sit on my bed, and we start making small talk. The topics changed with every word we said, and they felt lost to me. Honestly, I wasn't even paying much attention. My mind was more focused on him. His eyes were always on me, and not for one second did they focus on something else. His words were sensational, simple, and spoken with care. I savored every one of them.

"So, what's your story?" Matthew asks me at some point.

I raise an eyebrow. "What do you mean?"

"I mean that I want to get to know you. Who you are, what you like to do, and so on?"

I feel like smiling. *He's interested in knowing who I am!* I fight the urge to share every detail about me, not because he asked me, but because I want to. Still, I don't want it to be like this. I want to close the distance between us, lay my head on his lap, and let him play with my hair as I talk. I want our eyes to meet at some point and let him lean forward slowly until our lips meet.

"Hey, are you doing alright?" Matthew asks.

"What?"

"I asked if you're doing alright. You look like you spaced out or something."

I gulp. "I'm fine. I promise."

Matthew raises an eyebrow, but then says, "Okay then. So, are you going to share your story?"

I lift my shoulders. "I'm not sure where to begin."

"Then how about we each ask a question to the other and after they answer, we share our own answer."

I smile. "I like the way you think."

"Cool. I'll start. What's your favorite color?"

Simple and random, and no biggie. "Blue. Yours?"

"Green," he says. "Now you."

We go at this for a while, asking question after question and each one of us answering every one of them. I get to learn bits and pieces of him as we go along. Apart from his favorite color being green, he likes poetry, mainly Instagram poetry for how easy and simple it captures emotions. His favorite food is pizza, pepperoni with extra cheese. His favorite hobbies include hiking, reading, and, in his words, spontaneous adventures.

"Spontaneous adventures?" I ask him.

"Yeah," he says. "You know like going out with no plan and ending up doing something fun." He gives a few examples. For instance, he once went on a road trip with some friends and ended up at least three hundred miles away from home. What they did, he didn't say, and I didn't dare to ask him.

As we went along, my mind thought of possible questions that I could ask that could help me hint out that he likes guys. Sadly, nothing comes to mind, but either way, we're getting along so that's a good thing. Maybe I could do this some other time, probably when a topic regarding the gay community or something romantic enters the discussion. Yeah, that'd be good. That way he won't get suspicious.

At some point Matthew asks, "If you could do anything right now, what would it be?"

If I could do anything right now. The words ring in my head. There's only one thing I'd like to do right now, and that's confess my feelings to him. I want to tell him how he makes me feel, and I want him to tell me that he feels the same way. I want him to take me in his arms, hug me, and kiss me. I want to be loved, cherished, cared for. I want him to be mine.

But I can't. If my parents—and his parents, if they're like mine—find out, who knows what'll happen to me, or us if he feels the same way. They'd probably separate us, ship us to different places, or who knows what. They'd force us to abandon each other, all under the illusion that it's wrong and that we should find ourselves some girls to be with. But I don't want that.

I want him. He took my heart and now I want him to keep it.

I reply, "I'm not sure."

"Come on," he says. "You've got to want something."

My dad's expression comes back into my mind. If he ever found out the truth, he would do everything I fear he would do, and even though I don't want to risk it, I still want to do it. Matthew is still waiting for an answer. He's probably wondering what's taking me so long. I take a deep breath and say, "I guess… I guess I would like to be free."

Matthew raises an eyebrow. "What do you mean by that?"

No turning around, my mind tells me. A part of me

wants to say everything, that I'm gay, I like him and that I'm afraid that if my parents find out they'll do who knows what. Instead, I say, "I mean that I'd like to be able to make my own decisions, free from my parents' control."

"Your parents control your decisions?"

"Not exactly," I say. "It's more like they want me to become someone I'm not."

Matthew raises his eyebrows. "How so?"

This is your chance, my mind tells me. *Tell him the truth and be out about it.* "I feel like all my life, I've been following their rules and doing what they ask. Now, I think that I only did that to make them happy rather than because I agreed with their rules. I feel like I've been acting like someone I'm not and whenever I try to open up about who I am, they shut me down. Because of that, I sometimes feel like I'm trapped, as if I were in a cage or chained up. Every time I open up about myself, it's me trying to get free, but it's like they don't want me to."

Matthew doesn't say anything. He looks at me, *studies* me, and then gets up from his seat and sits right beside me. Him being so close sends a chill through my spine. I can barely control it. My hands are rested on my knees, and my head is lowered. I avoid his eyes. God only knows what he might find behind them, maybe the truth, which scares me a lot.

For a few seconds, Matthew does nothing. He stays seated right beside me and doesn't even look at me. At some point, he extends a hand and grabs mine. His hand is warm, and his fingers intertwine with mine. He holds it gently, but reassuringly, like if he was trying to tell me that he's here for me.

I like it.

Matthew opens his mouth. "Sometimes, I feel like my dad wants me to become like him," he says. "I feel like he's been prepping me to become the new him so that I may carry on the family beliefs and to spread the Word. I feel like I can't escape it, just like you. But here's the thing; I can. *We* can. It can happen later on or now, and if it's now, I can confidently tell you it's possible."

His words... shock me. All this time, I thought that he was just like his father: fully devoted to God and all that stuff. But my theory of him was actually true. He's like me: a boy who's trapped in the world in which he was born, dreaming of the day he can escape. I look into his eyes, and I see it. The fire that I saw in him is burning slowly, but brightly. He thinks it's possible for us to escape now.

And I have a feeling that he's right.

I look into his eyes and smile. He smiles back. My heart warms and my breath shortens up. I feel like kissing him. I *want* to. I want to press my lips to his, feel their warmth, savor their taste. Strangely enough, I find myself leaning forward to him.

I come to my senses and before I plant my lips on his, I plant my head on his shoulder. He wasn't doing the same thing I was. This was damage control. *Idiot*, my mind tells me. I ignore it. Matthew lifts his other arm and hugs me gently, but with the same care as when he held my hand. "Thank you," I tell him.

Matthew looks down at my head and smiles. "No problem," he says.

He wraps an arm around my head, and I let the feeling of his fingers running through my hair sink in.

4

Matthew's family leaves right after dinner, which brings me relief because I no longer have to be on guard at all times. As soon as they've taken off, I head upstairs to go to sleep, but my mind doesn't cooperate.

As I lie in bed, thoughts ramble through my brain. What mainly runs through it is how Matthew and I had a moment—or whatever that was. I feel like an idiot for leaning into him like that. Thankfully, I had a backup plan, and it seems that he didn't take notice of how I wanted to kiss him. Still, a part of me wanted to do it.

Maybe he would've liked it. Our lips would touch, and he would kiss me back, softly at first, then a little bit stronger. He'd raise his arms and pull me closer, and I'd do the same to him. He'd stroke my back as we kiss, spreading his fingers out to take up as much of it as he could. We'd lay down on my bed at some point, our lips never separating and keeping close to one another. Our eyes would be closed, but only because we're enjoying the moment. There wouldn't be a need to look at each other.

Now I can't help myself. I picture us going further. The kissing intensifies just as his tongue slips into my mouth. I savor its taste and he moves it around in there in search of mine. He stops kissing me and moves on to my neck and shoulders. He starts to loosen my shirt; I do the same and our bare chests converge in a sea of passion and excitement. The heat from his skin is intoxicating.

We loosen our pants; he unzips mine while I do his. We throw them aside and our legs tangle as we keep kissing. His hands run across my back and a moment comes where he squeezes my butt and licks my chin. I groan. He goes down lower, kissing my neck, my chest, and my stomach. He reaches my underwear, kisses in between my legs and proceeds to pull them down. He runs a hand through my thigh, and then—

My body reacts. I can't stop it. Excitement flows through me and before I can react, I ejaculate in my underwear. *Fuck*, I tell myself. I jump out of bed and head for the bathroom.

Thankfully, mom and dad are already asleep. When I get to the bathroom, I lock the door, take off the underwear and scrub off the cum with running water. Once I'm done, I dry them up and examine them. It doesn't seem so bad, so I can still wear them. It's a good thing I got to work fast.

I think about what just happened. There's a first for everything but fantasies like that are something I'm not used to. I've had them before, bits and pieces of what could happen, but never like this. So clear and precise. I knew exactly what I wanted, and I wanted to do it with him.

I think of what I imagined and what could've happened if I continued. There are so many things that I want him to do to me, and so many things I want to do to him. Apart from what I've thought of, I think of the action, the heat, the hours we'd spend at it. I think of how we'd finish up and lie in bed, naked and tired, wrapped around each other under the sheets. I picture us there, his arms around me, my back pressed to his chest, his head next to mine. I picture a small conversation, an exchange of simple words, all in between the lines of "I love you" and "I never want to leave your side."

I want all that to happen. I want him. I want him to be mine and mine only. He already took my heart, and I don't care what challenge comes in between us. I'm still going to fight to get what I want, even if that fight involves facing my parents.

I lie back in bed, and thankfully, I don't fantasize again. Instead, I think of past moments, small and big hints that told me I was gay.

I think back to the seventh-grade community service activity where I went to a help clean up a beach not too far from town. I remember picking up trash from the sand when I spotted two men kissing under the palm trees. They were like any other pair of lovebirds: happy and in love. I watched them in awe. After some time passed, they kept on walking, and I went back to picking up trash. I never thought about it after that.

I think back to being in the locker room after gym class in eighth grade. I remember how one of my classmates was standing near the sinks when he took his shirt off. I've seen the others without their shirts as well, but none of them could be compared to him. His chest was buffed up and his arms were lean and cut.

The sweat made his body shine, as if he were covered in oil. I watched as he flexed his muscles in front of the mirror for a few seconds before my body responded. I turned away in panic, but not before I noticed myself getting hard.

I think that was when I started to deny it. I pushed it down somewhere deep where it stayed buried for some time. Then came Kylie Monroe's closet, when Nora and I made out in the darkness. I remember closing my eyes, doing everything I could think of that wasn't over the line and thinking to myself, *If I just keep doing this with her, everything will be alright. I may have thoughts about boys, but I can still like girls.* That was an excuse I used to deny it. If it wasn't for our talk after that, I would've probably kept going like that.

In a way, I guess I've always known what I wanted, but I never tried to pursue it. There was never anyone to tell me that it was normal, and no one ever talked about it. To be honest, it took my own personal research to knew what it meant to be gay, and time to accept that I identified with the definition. I'm not ashamed. Still, after coming out, a part of me wonders if I should've stayed closeted.

A part of me wants to believe that this is a story

that'll end with *happily ever after.* I still like to think that I'll get through the bad and it'll all work out in the end. No matter how many times I tell myself this, though, only half of me thinks it will happen. My dad is an asshole who literally slapped me after I told him everything, so he'll be a challenge. My mom seems unsure of what she thinks of it, but after that moment in my room, I think she'll warm back up to me. Still, I need to tread carefully as I think of a next step. One wrong move could end it all.

I consider leaving, packing up a bag and running away from home. Go to Nora's maybe, Alex's if not. They always said they'd help me if I needed it. Still, I couldn't. Dad would track me down and force me back, and I can't leave Mom. She may not show it, but I think she's trying to accept me. She seems to *want* to. What does that say about me if I don't let her try?

I want to escape, but there doesn't seem to be a way. Matthew believes we can escape, and it seems like he did. He's still here, but he found a way to break free from his father's control. I saw it within him, a secret part of him his father doesn't know. A beautiful secret.

I want that, and I think Matthew can help me get it.

5

I first see Matthew on Monday when he's called by the homeroom teacher to introduce himself to the classroom. He stands up, shares a few details about himself. We're told to make him feel welcome. After that, I don't see him until third period when he comes into the classroom as we were about to begin our discussion of Macbeth. My focus was mainly on Matthew, who paid close attention to the discussion, even adding his own opinion. The way he spoke made it sound like he's read it carefully, taking every detail, analyzing it, making his own conclusions. He only looked at me once and when our eyes met, he smiled at me. My heart melted.

I don't see him anywhere after that. When lunchtime arrives, I take the chance to look for him through the hallways on my way to the cafeteria, but the mob of students heading the same direction didn't give me a window to spot him. Knowing I probably won't see him until the school day ends, I quit my search and fall in line to get some food.

I settle for my usual ham and cheese sandwich and a bottle of water. Once it's all in my hands, I head over to sit down with Alex and Nora. It's easy to know where they are because, knowing them, they'd be sitting on the bench in the courtyard, near the tree that provides good shade, our spot. It's preferable to the cafeteria; we sit there because we get to enjoy the full hour of fresh air and sunshine before we go back to the classroom. It's the least crowded spot during lunchtime because most kids stay in the cafeteria or go to the basketball court.

I come out of the cafeteria and march into the courtyard. Nora and Alex are already there when I arrive. Nora is sitting under the tree with her back resting against the trunk, chowing down on the last piece of her sandwich. She holds her phone in one hand, scrolling through Instagram. Alex sits on the bench and crosses his legs as he swallows the last slices of an orange. Right beside him sits a closed notebook with a page marked by a pencil. He's probably studying for something.

Both of my friends eye me as I approach them. Alex

smiles, and I smile back. I sit next to him and unwrap my sandwich to take a bite, gazing at my friends. Neither says a word. Alex looks at me for a second and then turns to Nora. Nora eyes him before she turns back to me.

I swallow. "What's going on?" I ask.

"Nothing," Nora replies. I know her well enough to know that she's lying. I eye her sternly, and then she rolls hers and says, "Alright, fine. Alex and I are worried about you."

I raise an eyebrow. "Why are you worried about me?"

Nora doesn't answer, but after one stern look from me, she says, "Okay, don't panic, but it's your parents. Mainly your dad. Alex said that he spotted your dad talking to Mr. Bartow and asking questions about the conversion clinic where Kyle is."

Naturally, I panic. "Did he—"

"Mention you," Nora breaks in. "No, he didn't. He was very discreet about it. He asked him how his son was doing and a whole bunch of other questions, mainly connected to what treatments they were giving him and if they're working."

Shit, I tell myself. *Shit, shit, shit!* My anxiety kicks

in. I can't think of any way of calming down or finding a solution. I can only imagine the worst.

I think I know what happens to people who go to the clinic. Either my parents take me to the clinic, or a van is sent to pick me up. They leave me there and I'm locked up for God knows how long—days, weeks, months, years. They pump me full of drugs and give electroshock treatments until I slowly lose my mind. I try to hold on to the thin chance that I'll get out, but I lose hope as time passes. I lose touch with the outside world and possibly even reality. Maybe I end up not being able to take it anymore, so when I get the chance, I take my life.

I shake those thoughts away and focus on good things: the sound of waves crashing, the morning sunrise, Matthew. *Matthew.* The thought of him calms me a little bit. I imagine him coming for me, as if he were some knight in shining armor. He shows up at the clinic and by some grand miracle, he gets me out of that hellhole. He takes me in his arms, puts me in a car and we drive away, not to his parents' house or mine, but somewhere else. A place where we could be free together.

I imagine what I'd say to him. *My savior, my hero,*

my love. A night comes when I wake up crying and he pulls me with into his arms and holds me tight. He whispers into my ear, tells me it's okay, and that he's here now. A tear rolls down my cheek. He kisses it away. We eye each other and smile. He runs a hand over my cheek before—

"Taylor," Alex says, pulling me out of my thoughts.

I blink a few times before I turn to him saying, "Yeah?"

"You were gone, dude. You looked like you spaced out or something. Are you okay?"

I nod gently, but to be honest, I'm not sure. If my dad is already asking about conversion therapy, then it means that the odds of him *not* sending me away are slim, so I'm practically doomed. I remember the look he gave me when he wasn't very happy that we were up alone in my room. "Nothing happened," I told him, but he didn't trust me. *Fall in line*, I tell myself. *Do what he asks; it might buy you some time.* I may be stretching my luck as much as my beliefs, but it's either that or give up and head to the clinic.

"You're thinking about it, aren't you," Nora tells me.

"What?" I ask her.

"Don't play dumb. You and I both know what you're thinking. Let me just say that your parents may not accept you, but they don't strike me as the type to send you away just like that."

"That's what you think, but you don't exactly see what's happening behind the curtain."

Nora understands what I mean by that. I like to think of life as this stage where everyone—myself included—is playing some sort of role in this world. In my case, I have to play the loyal son who'll do what his father says, even if it denies me my own happiness. It's the only thing I can do, or else he can send me off like Kyle's parents did with him. But I'm buying time, making preparations to try and fix things.

I just need to be careful.

Nora pulls me back into the conversation. "So why don't you explain it to us?" she asks. "Why don't you tell us what really happens behind the curtain?"

I give her a stern look. "Do I look like I'm in the mood to share?"

"I'm afraid you don't have a choice," she replies. "If you want us to help you, you need to open up."

I turn to Alex, who gives me a look that tells me that he agrees with her. I let out a sigh. Why is it that

I always feel like they stand together when the conversation is about me? Any time the subject regards something about my life—school, family, crushes—they push me into sharing by either not saying anything or pushing me into the spotlight. Sometimes I manage to get out of it, and sometimes I don't.

This time it's the latter.

I take a deep breath. "I just…" My voice falters. I try again but nothing comes out. I lower my head. Shame flares up inside me. I shrink.

Alex reacts quickly. He takes my hand and squeezes it gently. Then he says, "It's okay. You don't need to speak. We get it."

I scoff. They definitely don't get it. They're not like me. They don't know what it's like to feel different, to feel like you don't fit in or know where your place is. They don't know what it's like to have your own parents turn against you and look at you differently simply because you don't agree with their view of things.

That's why they tend to hate people like me; I don't fit into their norms. I don't fit what they were taught that was expected of them. It's a blessing and a curse.

I look at Alex in the eye. "Thank you," I say gently. Alex nods gently and then let's go of my hand. Right now, these two people are the only ones who have my back. I can't risk losing them.

"Okay," Nora said. "Since you won't tell us about your home situation, why don't you tell us about Matthew?"

My eyes widen. I turn to Alex who looks at me and says, "Yeah. Nora filled me in, but I'm curious as to what you have to say."

I look at him with shock. He knew, all this time, and he just didn't say anything! I turn to Nora, who looks at me with a smirk. I scowl. "Don't look at me like that," she tells me. "You told me something huge and you thought I was going to keep it from Alex." She shakes her head.

I roll my eyes. "There's nothing to tell, honestly."

"Liar," Nora says. "I see it in your eyes. Something happened. Come on. Tell us."

I groan. I look at Alex, who raises his shoulders and mouths a little please. "Nothing happened, I swear."

"Well, something must've happened between you two, considering he's walking over here as we speak."

Nora points a finger to the distance and when I turn around, I see Matthew walking towards us. His hair is in the same curly state as yesterday. His eyes are hidden behind a pair of glasses, which to be honest, makes him look good, in a nerdy kind of way. He's holding a book in one hand; a simple hardcover with a few words imprinted on it. As he nears us, I turn to Nora, then Alex. "She met him at her biology class and said that she could hook him up with you during lunch," he whispers to me.

"Please tell me she didn't really say it like that."

Alex doesn't answer. Matthew gets to us and says, "Hi," a little quiet, but clear to understand. I smile and give him a little wave. He turns to me and says, "Hey, Taylor. I've been looking for you."

My heart melts. He's been looking for me! I don't respond, but after a little hit from Alex's elbow, I say, "Really? I mean, yeah. I was looking for you too."

"Oh, you were?"

I nod. "I was looking to see if you wanted to sit with us during lunch, but I couldn't find you anywhere." "Oh, I was waiting for the line to go down at the library."

"Cool," I say.

"Yeah, I sort of got lost while I was reading so now there's nothing to eat."

I look down at my lap. The other half of my ham

and cheese sandwich sits there untouched. I pick it up and say, "You can have this if you want."

"Oh no. I couldn't."

"It's okay. I'm not that hungry."

Matthew's eyes study me. Then he smiles. "If you insist."

I hand it to him, and I can feel Nora and Alex's eyes on me. Alex is probably keeping whatever he's thinking to himself. He never liked to meddle in other people's personal business. Nora definitely will have a smirk on her face. She's probably thinking, *Oh yeah. Real smooth.* I resist the urge to roll my eyes.

Matthew examines the sandwich in his hand. Then he raises it up to his mouth and takes a bite. He chews a bit, and once he swallows, he says, "It's really good."

I smile. He looks at me and smiles back. Alex and Nora watch keenly. Nora's lips curve into a smile. I see the excitement hiding behind it. She's been my friend for so long, and she's always known how lonely I felt. She always hoped that when I'd find someone, he would find a way to lift me out of my sorrows and help me shine. Maybe she sees what I see, or maybe even more.

"Hey, do you wanna maybe hang out after school?" Matthew asks.

"What?" I ask, turning my head to him.

"I asked if you wanted to hang out. I've got no plans after school and to be honest, I think you're a great guy, so yeah. I thought we could hang out or something."

He wants me to hang out with him. He wants me to hang out with him! I hold down my excitement. I turn to Nora, who gives me a slight nod. In my heart, I want to say yes, but my head is telling me that I should say no. I look at Matthew. "Well, the truth is that—"

"What he means to say is yes," Nora breaks in. "He doesn't have anything planned for today after school so he's practically free."

I raise an eyebrow at Nora. Since when did she become my own personal matchmaker? I mean, she did this once with me back in third grade, which I will add, didn't end well and she hasn't done that with anyone since. Maybe it's because of what she said back then. "Because you might as well be a hopeless case," she had said. I don't think it was because of that. I think it was because I never felt connected to the people she matched me with.

Yet here I have a chance. And all I have to say is one thing.

"If you don't want to go or if you have plans, we can

hang out some other time," Matthew tells me.

I take this chance. "No," I say. "Let's hang out after school."

Matthew's lips curve into a smile, but I think that he's holding back the urge to have it wider. "Great. Meet me after school by the front gate. I gotta go." He turns around and walks away.

"Wait," I say a little loud, but I calm myself and say, "What are we going to do?"

Matthew turns to me and smiles. "Let me surprise you," he says, and keeps on walking.

He's gone before I can say something else. Something about his reply makes it sound mysterious. It terrifies me a little, but it also fills me with joy. He asked me to hang out with him and he wants to surprise me! I am ecstatic. I feel like jumping up and down and dancing like a fool.

Matthew and I are hanging out.

6

I meet Matthew after school by the front gate as planned. When the final bell rings, I pick up my stuff, put any books I don't need in my locker, and race through the hallway to the main entrance. Matthew is already there, sitting on a bench near the gate with his eyes glued to a book. He mouths the words as he reads. A moment comes where he lifts his head up a little, and the sunlight touches his cheeks, brightening them. He looks angelic. My heart melts.

My mind floats back to what Nora told me after he left. "He totally likes you," she had said. I rolled my eyes. I told her that just because he invited me to hang out doesn't mean that he likes me. "You didn't see it," she said back. "You didn't see how he looked at you and how he smiled when you said yes. He likes you, and you can't see it because you're too busy worrying."

Truth be told, she's right. I am worried. If my dad catches me hanging out with him, I'm toast. He already has the idea of sending me to conversion therapy in mind and I'm not interested in poking him hard enough to see if he'll do it. Thankfully, I have a cover. I texted mom that I'll be hanging out with Nora after school, and she said it was okay. Nora will keep up the ruse for as long as she can. It won't be much trouble since mom likes Nora, but if anything happens, I know she'll make sure to call me.

I need to make sure that I'm back before nightfall. Dad's rules, not mine. I have three hours before the sun sets, so I better make the best of it.

I walk over to Matthew as he starts packing his stuff. Once I'm close enough, he looks at me and smiles. "There you are," he says. "You ready?"

A part of me thinks that I should cancel. I should tell him that something came up and I can't hang out. Then the other part tells me that I should go with him because if I don't, I won't know when another shot like this will come. I feel light, as if I were full of air. I want to smile. I do, a little, but I make sure not to get carried away. "Yeah," I say. "Let's go."

Matthew puts his backpack on his shoulder. "Follow me," he says, and we head off.

We leave the school grounds and walk, a lot. We go through several streets and leave the suburban area where our school is at and head into Main Street. Our surroundings change from an endless number of houses all around us to small buildings with a maximum of five stories. We pass through sights that are familiar to me—the art store that always has some paintings done by the employees hung on display; the pizzeria that has that old brick oven that puffs smoke out from the roof; the diner where Nora, Alex and I usually go together after school on Fridays to chow down on some burgers and milkshakes. All of it is… just perfect, maybe a little too much, but still perfect.

Matthew is the one who leads us. Despite him still being new here, he seems to know his way around town. He guides us through the urban streets without once stopping to look around or ask for directions. I watch him as we go. "How do you know where we're going?" I ask.

Matthew looks back to me. "I went exploring a little bit yesterday," he said. "Thought I'd get to know my new home."

"Where did you go?

He smiles. "You'll see."

His movements are calm and simple, he is not in a rush like I usually am. A moment comes when we pass through a light post by a corner and he wraps an arm on the pole and swings himself around it, smiling and giggling. I smile a little bit, mainly to hide my worry.

I'm not worried about being with him. I'm glad that I'm with him but being with him in public is a risk. My dad moves around town, as part of his work as a consultant. He mostly works from home, but on a few occasions he's here on Main Street in his office. If he were to catch us together, he might grow suspicious and then my nightmare would become a reality. I keep an eye out for him, silently praying that he isn't around. There's no sign of him, but I'm not letting my guard down.

"Hey, are you okay?" Matthew asks me. He stopped swinging around the pole. A look of worry has replaced the smile on his face.

I turn to him. "Yeah," I say.

"Are you sure? You seem a little worried and you keep looking around as if you're worried about seeing someone. Is something up?"

My throat tangles up. Matthew keeps looking at me in the eye, waiting for me to answer. My heartbeat kicks up. Sweat fills up my palms and I feel like I'm about to pass out. I take a deep breath. "Yeah, I'm okay. Promise."

Matthew raises an eyebrow, but he doesn't say a thing. All he does is smile, and we keep on walking.

We walk a little bit more until we finally stop at the corner bookstore.

It's one of those places that brings a person comfort when they walk in. Every time I step in here, it's the same feeling of security that comes to me. When we walk inside, we're welcomed by the charming sound of a pair of small bells that hang by the door. The next thing that comes is the soulful tunes of sweet jazz playing on the speakers of the store. The scene is like any other bookstore; it's a room filled with shelves of books of all genres, titles, ages, and sizes. A pair of couches and tables sit near the windows, where three people are seated. Dozens of smells fill the air, some familiar, some not, each originating from a different place and with a different meaning to it.

Matthew sets his backpack down on the couch. I

do the same and then I look at him and say, "So, your exploring brought you to the bookstore?"

Matthew nods. "It's a good place to explore."

"If you say so. So, what are we doing here?"

Matthew smiles. "I figured we could hang out somewhere where we could go wherever we want."

I raise an eyebrow. "What do you mean by that?"

He gestures to the bookshelves. "Don't you ever think of books as gateways to different realms? I mean think about it, you open a book, and you instantly step into a world that someone else created. You could become anyone by reading, and the best part is that you can find yourself through it. Come on."

I don't get a chance to object. He takes my hand and pulls me into the maze of bookshelves. As quickly as we came in, we dive into the shelves. The light of day dissipates as we dive deeper, leaving only the cold fluorescent lights of the ceiling as the only thing letting us see. The sound of the jazz song gets lower. There are never any speakers deeper in the maze. The scent of paper fills my lungs.

None of that distracts me from the shockwave of excitement that's spreading through me. He's grabbed my hand and I'm liking it. I smile a little bit. Matthew takes notice of it and smiles back. My smile widens.

We cross through the different sections of books—classics, thrillers, horror, sci-fi, romance—until we stop in a small room located in a corner of the shop. In it lies a couple of shelves that only reach as high as my stomach, most of them not even half-full. In a corner lie two beanbags with a little nightstand in between them. An antique typewriter rests on top of it. Bistro lights hang from the walls, lighting up the space to the fullest. A magenta neon sign shaped like the word "love" hangs below them. A carpet covers most of the wooden floor.

There's no one else in this part of the store. Just he and I.

"This is the poetry section," Matthew tells me. "Not many people know of this area and the few who do need to ask for directions to find it."

I look at him. Part of his face is lit up by the neon sign. "I didn't even know this was here, or that it looked like this. It's nothing like the rest of the store."

"Yeah, well the owner wanted to remodel the area, so I offered him some pointers."

"Wait, you're the one who did all this?" I gesture to the room.

"Well, I told the owner what he should do, and it

looks like he took my advice. By what I can see, sales apparently went up for poetry books."

"I can see that, but why are we here?"

"I figured that if we were to transport to another realm, might as well start with poetry, specifically modern poetry."

"But why?"

Matthew's expression changes, in a positive way. "Well, yesterday I told you about how I'm into Instagram poetry and not just for how easy it is to understand, but because of how so few words can move me in so many ways. It made me feel like I've done things I've never done. It also made me think of feelings I've never felt before. I wanted to see if you would like to see what I'm talking about."

I smile gently. He wants to read poetry to me. He wants to read poetry to me! Is this a sign? Is he trying to tell me that he likes me? What other explanation can there be for this? Who reads poetry to a friend? "What poetry book would you suggest?" I ask him.

Matthew smiles. "Make your pick."

I eye the shelves. Even though there aren't many books in them, there are still plenty to choose from, each one ranging from a different topic and author. I look at the names. I don't recognize many of them, but it doesn't matter. The titles pique my interest. Some of them have the strangest names, but they're the ones that draw me in the most. I just can't decide.

I look at Matthew. "Do you have any suggestions?"

Matthew shakes his head. "I'm not the one who's going to be listening to me reading it. Just pick the one that calls to you the most."

His choice of words astound me. *Just pick the one that calls to you the most.* I turn to the books, every one of them seems to be calling me, but I don't think it's because I'm interested in them. It's more because I'd like to hear him read me its contents. I want to hear him pronounce every word, every syllable, every letter, and I want him to explain everything to me. I look at him and see how he waits for me to decide, patiently. I admire that.

Finally, I make a choice, more like a random one. I close my eyes and stretch out a hand to pick out a book. I run my fingers through the spines, then grab a hold of one and pull it out. I open my eyes and hand it to Matthew. He takes it in his hands, stares at the cover and says, "Good choice."

I smile gently. "So, are you going to read it to me?"

Matthew nods. "Sit."

I take a seat in a beanbag while Matthew sits in the other. He opens the book and after clearing his throat, he begins. He recites the lines with care and generosity, always speaking smoothly and making the occasional gesture with his hand at the right time. My focus gets lost within many things—the lines, the sound of Matthew's voice, his hand gestures—mostly things regarding Matthew. He sits right in front of me, reading the poetry book in his hand aloud to me. There's nowhere else I'd rather be.

There are the occasional moments where he stops looking at the text and looks at me. When he does that, he smiles gently. My heart melts every time. A moment comes when we look at each other again, and his expression changes. His smile fades and he places the book on his lap. I raise an eyebrow. "Is something wrong?" I ask him.

Matthew doesn't answer. He sets the book aside and eyes me longer, curiously. A tension builds inside me. He looks at me as if he is trying to find something. Maybe it's something else, something I'm not seeing. He looks like he's in the middle of a struggle, internal by the looks of it. But what's it about?

That's when Matthew does something I don't expect. As he keeps his eyes on me, he stretches a hand towards me and places it on top of my knee. I stare down at it. His hand is on my knee. His hand is on my knee! My body shakes. A breath slips out of my mouth.

He notices. "You okay?" he asks.

I don't answer. My mind is still taking in the fact that he's placed his hand on my knee. I enjoy it while it lasts. The pressure of his hand warms my skin. A sense of security flows through the touch. Could this be a sign? Could this be him telling me that he has a thing for me?

Should I make a move? I think I should. There's nothing worse than leaving someone confused as to whether you like them. What should I do? Should I speak or should I smile? God, this is all so complicated. *Do something now*, my mind screams at me.

Matthew slowly starts to pull his hand away from me. I act quickly. I take his hand into mine and hold it gently. Matthew stares down at the connection between us, and I don't stop there. I caress his hand with my thumb, and I feel Matthew's body shiver a little bit. Is he just as scared as I am? At least I know that there's something between us, something raw and pure, and waiting to grow into something greater.

Matthew looks at me, and I look at him. I smile gently and he smiles as well. The thought of kissing him comes to mind, but I don't dare to go forward with the idea. I'm still in the moment, caressing his hand in a room all alone. He either makes another move or tells me to stop, but we just sit here, quietly enjoying the comfort of each other's touch, neither of us wanting it to end. As far as I know, he likes it as much as I do, which makes me happy.

I don't feel time pass until Matthew looks down at his watch and tells me that we have to leave. And just like that, the moment ended as quickly as it began. Matthew puts the book away and I hoist my backpack on my shoulders. As we walk through the corridors, Matthew grabs me by the arm and yanks me back to him. "Can we hang out again?" he asks me, giving me puppy eyes and all.

"Yes," I reply, not bothering to think about it.

Matthew's smile widens, and I'm flooded with joy.

7

"So, tell me what happened!" Nora insists the second she sees me in the hallways. There's more to this than just wondering what happened. She probably wants to know every detail, including what I had done. I say nothing, to which she responds by eyeing me sternly and saying, "Your silent treatment isn't gonna work on me. Now, spill."

I roll my eyes and guide her into a classroom. I never liked having very private, sensitive conversations in the hallways, even if they are practically empty. We come into the classroom and sit all the way in the back. The teacher is in here as well, seated behind her desk looking down at some papers. She looks up at us when we walk in but doesn't say anything. She's looking back down at her papers as soon as we're in the back. That's good; that means I won't have to worry about her listening in.

Nora looks at me sternly. "So, what happened?" she asks again.

"Shhh." I place a finger between my lips to get her to lower her voice.

"Sorry," she says in a lower tone. "Seriously though. Tell me what happened."

I look at the teacher. She isn't paying attention, but she's well known for having good ears. I lean closer to her and whisper into her ear what happened, how Matthew and I went to the bookstore, how he took me to a secluded part and read poetry to me. Nora listened with care, not speaking until I was done. "You're leaving something out," she says. "I can tell that you are. It's written all over your face."

I bite my lip. "Well... he may have put his hand on my knee."

"And..." She gestures me to go on.

"And... I may have grabbed it. And caressed it. And accepted another invitation to hang out with him." Nora's eyes widen. "Wow," she whisper-shouts. "That was fast. I guess he doesn't want to take it slow."

"Hey, that may not have anything to do with him

liking me. Maybe he just likes spending time with me."

"Yeah, and so do I, but you don't see me reading poetry to you and putting my hand on your knee. The way you said it made it sound like he was making a move on you."

My cheeks turn red. Was he really making a move on me? I guess I wasn't seeing it. I was still lost at how I took his hand and how I caressed it gently. His skin felt warm on my hand, and really, really soft. His grip was gentle and when he asked me to hang out again, I blurted out a yes. I didn't bother giving it a thought—I was too into the moment that I didn't want to refuse.

Nora pats me on the shoulder. "Hey, this is good. It means that he's into you."

"Well… not necessarily. He hasn't said anything about that yet, so…"

She rolls her eyes. "Wow. You *really* are blind when it comes to signals or maybe you're just in denial." I raise an eyebrow. "What's that supposed to mean?"

The bell rings. Students start coming into the classroom and taking seats in any empty desks. Nora doesn't answer my question. She just picks her stuff up and says, "You know what I mean", which I do not. I push it aside and focus on the day.

Classes go by smoothly with the occasional discussions, schoolwork, and whatnot. I see Matthew at lunch. We sit in the courtyard alone, because Alex and Nora told me that they had to "study." We talk a bit and make new plans for after school.

Matthew wants to do homework with me at his house.

Matthew's family lives in a secluded farmhouse in the woods outside of town. Since I can't ask my parents for a ride out of fear of raising alarm, I'm left with only one option: walking. If that's not bad, try the idea of carrying a backpack full of books for at least an hour walk with no place to stop and rest. Within twenty minutes into the walk, my feet and back start to ache, but regardless, I press forward.

I get to his place around 4:30pm. By the time his house comes to view, my legs are tired and wobbly, my feet hurt, and I'm longing for the first chance I get to sit down. I head to the porch and ring the doorbell. He answers in less than a minute. He opens the door and smiles. "You're here," he says.

I nod.

"How are you?"

"Tired," I reply. "And my feet hurt."

Matthew laughs under his breath. "You think that's bad. Why don't you try doing that every day from Monday to Friday?"

"You do this *every* school day?" I say with my eyes wide open.

Matthew nods. "Today was an exception. My mom was on her way home to get something and so she picked me up. At least I don't have to walk to school. My mom drops me off before heading to work."

"If walking home is such a hassle, why did your parents decide to buy this place?"

"They love nature," he replies. "They had their doubts because of the walking distance I'd have to go through, but I convinced them that I was okay with it. Besides, I like the peace and quiet, and the solitude."

I raise an eyebrow. "The solitude?"

"Yeah. It's nice to hang around here when I'm alone. Gives me certain types of freedoms."

"What kinds of freedoms?"

Matthew doesn't answer. instead, he evades the question by saying, "How 'bout we go up to my room?" I'm curious as to why he does that, but don't bother in asking him about it. It was just some stupid small talk, not really important. He has his reasons. He gestures me to come on in, I do, and from there, we head up to his room.

His room is nothing out of the ordinary; there's a bed, a desk, a closet full of clothes; all the usual stuff. Still, it's special because it's his. This is his world, and it's him put out in an abundance of objects. Each one gives me a hint, from the green painted walls to the different photos taken from what seem like hiking trips he's been on. I spot a camera sitting on his dresser. I guess he likes to take photos.

His bookshelf catches my eye. Three shelves hang on the wall filled with more books than they can hold. There were so many of them that some had to be stacked like a tower placed on top of the ones lined up. I look at the names of the authors; he's got good taste. Some of the other books are from current authors that I know about and there are even some about Instapoetry.

Only one word comes out of my mouth: "Wow."

"Yeah," Matthew says from behind me. "I happen to read a lot."

I turn to him. "This is more than I've read in my entire life. Don't you ever get tired of reading?"

"I do, sometimes. Then I jump back into it and I'm

happy once again."

I smile. Something about him being a total book-worm is so… sexy. I find it hot and attractive. I find *him* attractive. I think this might be the first time I confess that. No. I've done that already, but only to myself, not to him.

I point to the photos. "Did you take those?"

Will scratches the back of his head. "Yeah. I like to snap shots of beautiful places."

"They look beautiful."

"Thanks." A minute of silence. "So, should we get studying?"

I nod gently and we begin. We sit side by side on his bed as we work. We only have one thing we can work on together—our English homework—which involves answering a series of questions regarding a part of our current reading assignment. When I ask Matthew about something, he pulls out his copy of Macbeth and skims through the pages in search of a quote that could help me develop an answer. When he finds one, he shows it to me, and I write it down along with a quick explanation about what it means.

We go at this for a while, and we occasionally talk, mainly about how our day was. I share a lot, but Matthew doesn't. When I ask him if he's made a few friends, he smiles at me and says that he has. Then I ask him if he's made any friends that aren't me and he shakes his head, which makes me feel bad for him. Now that I think about it, I don't ever see him hanging around anywhere during lunch except the library. Maybe I should invite him to hang out with me and my friends. They already like him, so maybe he'll like them as well.

We talk of other things, and I manage to bring up the topic of his photos. He pulls up a portfolio full of pictures to show to me. I have to admit, he's got a good eye. Each one is beautiful in the sense of its location, colors, and textures. The definition of the places makes them seem almost as if I'm looking at the real place. He tells me how he enjoys doing this and how he plans on finding a way to sell them. "I want people to see beauty in places," he says. "And if they can't see them for real, I want them to see them through my photos."

I want to say that I appreciate them, but that can wait.

We keep studying, answering question after question, until finally get to the last question. Matthew finds me a quote that he claims can be useful. When I write it down, he says, "What do you think it means?"

I look at him. "What?"

"The quote from Macbeth. The one where he tells his wife to be a flower on top but a serpent underneath."

Random, but hey, I'll bite. "I think it means that he wants her to hide her true intentions. They're planning to kill the king to get Macbeth to become a king faster and so that's a metaphor for giving off an innocent appearance, so the king doesn't suspect a thing."

Matthew smiles. "Nice." He stays quiet for a minute, but then he says, "Sometimes, I do that."

I raise an eyebrow. "What? Hide your true intentions."

"Yeah, I do. Occasionally, I do it to get something I want. Mainly it's to get some freedoms, but sometimes I have other things in mind."

My eyes widen a little. "Like what," I ask.

Matthew doesn't answer. He doesn't even look at me. He looks down at his feet, lost in some way. He opens his mouth but doesn't say a word. He closes it again and does nothing.

Now I can't help but look at him. His eyes look lost, yet so alive in some way. They give off the appearance that some weight was lifted off him. But what? What is he keeping hidden and why does it connect with him hiding his true intentions? I know now that he didn't invite me here just to study; I got that from his confession, if it was even a confession to begin with. *What are you hiding?* I ask myself.

I lean closer to him. My proximity makes him look at me. His lips curve into a smile. The feeling behind his eyes change. They no longer look lost.

They look… joyful.

"Do you—"

Before I can finish, Matthew leans into me, and presses his lips to mine. My eyes widen when I realize what is happening, letting warmth of his lips engulf me. After a few seconds, he slips his tongue into my mouth and presses it to mine. I start to kiss him back and begin to feel the joy through his lips. He wants to smile, but he'd rather keep kissing me, which to be honest, makes me happy because I don't want this to end.

The kiss intensifies. Normally, that would've already begun when we pressed our tongues together, but things kicked up a notch when he pulled me closer to him. Our chests converge and the mixture of body heat and saliva overwhelms me. We push each other back and forth until we end up lying down on his bed. He lays on top of me, and I run my hands up and down his back. At some point, my hand goes lower than I expected, and it lands on his butt. I squeeze it gently and he groans, and I pull him closer to me.

I want him in a whole other way now. I like what we're doing, but I want to go further. I might never get another chance, at least not for a while. I want to take a chance, but he might not be ready. Then again, he just kissed me, and we've only known each other for about three days. That's answers a few questions I had about him but brings up new ones that can wait for later.

What's happening now will define the rest.

We keep at this for a few more minutes until Matthew begins to drag his hands down to my pants. He pulls away for a second and asks me if I'm okay with this. I know what he means by that; it's practically written by his actions. To be honest, I want him to keep at it. We might be jumping a few steps forward, but I want this as much as he does. I nod gently and he smiles. Then he proceeds to unzipping my pants and bending down over me.

Matthew takes it easy on me, going back and forth slowly with his hands running through my thighs. His face is resting in between my legs. I wrap them around him and pull him inwards. He raises his hands up to my stomach while mine went to play around with his hair, which he happened to like. Matthew's enjoying every second of it. He gave out a few gasps and moans along with the occasional sucking sound, and he never stopped. I liked it as well, and I showed it with every gasp and moan that came out of my mouth and whatever moves I made as well.

Once he's done, Matthew picks up a blanket from the side and covers us up to our chests. For a while we lay in silence, and my mind tries to grasp all that has happened as I keep panting. I gaze at the ceiling. Nothing's on it, but there's nothing else to see, and I don't even dare to turn my head to look at him. I feel Matthew's eyes on me, studying the look on my face. I can already tell what he's thinking, and it's proven with what he says. "Was it too much?"

I turn to him. "No," I say gently.

"Then why do you look traumatized or something?

I bite my lip. "I guess... because this is all new to me."

"Did you at least enjoy it?"

I tilt my body and place a hand on his chest. Matthew grabs it and then pulls me in until my head is resting on his chest. He kisses me on the forehead, and then I raise my head and press my lips to his. We go at this for a while, kissing each other back and forth with our hands running all over the other. I hoist myself on top of him and proceed to slipping my tongue into his mouth.

"You want it too, don't you?" I say to him.

Matthew looks into my eyes. "Well, I do, but you don't have to. I honestly didn't expect this to happen."

I raise an eyebrow. "You didn't?"

"I mean, I did, but not today, and so soon. I just figured I'd kiss you and then we'd talk about the whole thing. You know, ask each other questions like 'How long have you known', 'Does anybody else know', and all that stuff. Then, things kicked up a notch and I wanted to do more. I was actually surprised that you didn't turn me down."

I small laugh escapes from my lips. "I was surprised as well. Was this your first time?"

Matthew nods.

"How did it feel?"

He smiles. "Good, honestly. I was actually afraid that you might not like it since I've never had practice, but all in all, it was good."

I lean in and move closer to his ear. "Want me to

make it even better?" I whisper into his ear.

I move away to see his smile widening. "What do you have in mind?" he asks.

I kiss him in many places—his lips, his neck, his shoulders—before proceeding to move down to his chest and thighs.

8

I carry the insanely odd yet pleasurable taste of his dick in my mouth all the way home. I don't bother with brushing my teeth or using mouthwash when I'm home. I let the flavor sink into my tongue and enjoy this memento of our intimacy for as long as I can. Once I have dinner and brush my teeth for the night, the taste is completely gone, which to be honest makes me feel a little bit sad since I don't know when or if we'll ever do that again. But even still, I can recall its feeling, and the memory of everything that happened before, during, and after I went down on him.

That night, my mind kept playing tricks with me. Every time I closed my eyes, I was dreaming that I was next to Matthew, naked and exposed, and I imagined us doing all sorts of stuff. Good news is that I didn't cum like the last time but thinking about the whole thing made me think of how I wanted more from that experience. I didn't get a chance to see if we could go further. We were both so tired that when I finished, we spent the rest of the time lying next to each other talking until it was time for me to go. He did at least give me a goodbye kiss, but he didn't say that he loved me or anything, which did disappoint me. I guess I was expecting that from that moment on, we would like… be in a relationship or something.

Maybe we still will be or maybe that's just wishful thinking. I'm not sure. What exactly did he want from me?

I try to figure that out but dose off in the process. Morning comes within the blink of an eye, and I hoist myself out of bed and dive into the shower. The hot water gives me the extra push I need to wake up. It was then that I thought about Matthew. I picture him waiting in the other room, and then I come in, wearing a towel or some jeans, and he smiles at me. He grabs my hand and presses the other one to my chest right where my heart is at. Then he leans forward to kiss me and we—

I stop myself, but it's a little too late. When I look

down, I notice how I'm already half hard. I close my eyes and think of everything that I could imagine—flowers, puppies, a long AP History class discussion—until it finally goes away. When I come out of the shower, I dry myself up and brush my teeth. Occasionally, my mind slips out of reality and goes back to Matthew's room, where we go at it again. I snap out of it again, but it's hopeless. I want to do it again, and I want to do it now.

It's way too early to think about that, I tell myself, but I don't want to stop. Since the day we first met, all I think about is him, and after yesterday, the idea of going at least half an hour without thinking of him seems like an impossibility.

Maybe I just need to get things straightened out. Yeah, that's what I need. Just a day or two where I think things over and figure out what this means. Matthew kissed me, and I kissed him. It means we both like each other, but there's no telling whether he wants more than that. I do, but he hasn't said anything. All that can wait. For now, I'm going to try to just process this.

I come into my room and notice my phone screen on. I pick it up and see a message from Matthew.

Matthew: Hey Taylor. It's Matthew. Is this you?

A part of me wants to ignore the text and take a break from thinking about him, but if I do that, it might make him think that I'm avoiding him. I pick up the phone.

Me: Yeah, it's me. How did you get my number?

Matthew: The class chat. You didn't give me your number yesterday, so I went into it and scrolled down until I found the one that had an icon with a photo of you on it.

Me: Hmm. Smart.

Me: So what's up?

Matthew: Not much really. Just wanna see how you're doing.

Me: <<raised eyebrow emoji>>

Matthew: Ok, fine. I wanted to see if we should talk about what happened yesterday.

Me: If you're having some regrets, then yeah. I think we should.

Matthew: Well, I'm not. Are you?

Me: No. I really wanted that. If I didn't, why would I let you go forward, and then do it to you?

Matthew: I don't know. It's just I've never done this before and, to be honest, I was surprised when you did it to me.

Me: Why?

Matthew: Because I've literally gone down on you when I've only known you for like less than a week! I've thought of the idea of doing this for a while, but I didn't think it would be so soon. I was actually surprised that you let me go ahead and do it.

Me: I was surprised that you kissed me first. I've been trying to figure out if you were into guys since we first met and that caught me by surprise.

Matthew: So does that mean that you've been into me since we met?

I bite my lip but keep writing.

Me: Yes.

Matthew: Wow. Well, just so you know, I like you too.

Matthew: You're cute, charming, nice, and sexier than I imagined.

Me: You really think so?

Matthew: Definitely.

Me: God, I'm blushing. <<blush emoji>>

Matthew: Well, I'm glad 'cause I'm telling you the truth. You're a really nice guy and I'm glad that we met.

Me: <<smiling emoji>>

Matthew: Btw, I'm dying to see you again. Think we can hang out soon?

I smile at the idea. We could go back to his house again. He was right about the solitude being good and it's a good place to be able to talk to him. The trouble is my parents. They might start wondering why I'm spending so much time out, and my dad would put two and two together. Matthew knows about my situation at home. I told him about it, and he told me about his situation with his parents.

"They don't know and it's probably for the best if they don't," he told me, which makes me think about how I came out and how I probably would have been better off keeping my mouth shut.

> **Me:** I think it's a bit risky that we keep meeting this much. We've already hung out twice in one day. My parents might get suspicious.
> **Me:** How 'bout we hang out during lunch? I could introduce you to my friends.
> **Matthew:** Do they know about us?
> **Me:** They know I'm into you, but nothing at all about you or what happened yesterday. We can tell them that we like each other. But the rest stays between us.
> **Matthew:** Ok, then. I'll see you at school.

I send Matthew a thumbs up emoji along with a waving hand emoji and I head out the door. The introduction of Matthew to Nora and Alex can be a good way to see how good of a person he is. Nora has a way of knowing is someone is bad news, and she definitely seems like she wants to get to know him. Alex would meet him just for me. He's always been there to keep me hopeful, and he'd be really happy to get to know him. He's mentioned it more than once. Guess he'll finally get his wish.

I get to the school grounds, and I run into Alex five minutes later. He's sitting in a bench on the hallway, a notebook open on his lap as he reads through his notes. He looks at me and we exchange a hello, then I proceed to sit next to him. For a while, we stay quiet. Like me, Alex isn't good at starting a conversation. It's only after three minutes that Alex says, "So what did you guys do?"

I know immediately what he's talking about, which I hoped he would not bring up. "What do you mean?" I ask him.

"You know my mom is friends with yours and according to her, she says that you came home a few hours late. So, you must've been at his house for a while."

I give it a thought. Was I really there for so long? I didn't notice. I was busy being into the moment. "His house is literally in the middle of nowhere so it's a long walk without a car or a bike."

Alex looks at me sternly. "Dodging the question doesn't work on me or Nora. You know that."

"And don't you know that I might not be telling the truth because it's personal?"

"Why would you keep quiet about going to his house when—" Alex stops talking. He looks at me for a second, studies my face, and then his eyes widen. "What did you do?"

"Nothing," I say oddly with a smile.

"Really? Because from what I can see, your cheeks are turning red and so it was definitely not nothing."

I bite my lip. Somehow, I can still feel the warmth of his lips on them. Thinking about them makes me want to smile. I fight the urge. Even still, I feel a shiver running through my spine. Alex has his eyes on me. I avoid them and lower my head.

A moment comes when I turn to him. He looks me in the eyes, then his eyes widen. "Did you... kiss him?"

That's when I feel my cheeks turn red. Sweat starts to fill my palms. I bit my lip even harder. Another shiver runs through my spine. I can tell that Alex noticed, but he doesn't bring it up. He doesn't say anything either. He just waits for me to answer.

"It was actually he who kissed me."

"Taylor," he exclaims.

"Keep it down," I tell him. "Someone could hear us."

"Sorry," he whispers. "It's just... wow. I didn't expect that."

"Well, now you know. End of story."

At that point, Matthew walks by and looks at us, mainly me. He gives me a gentle smile and is gone before I can smile back at him. Alex looks at me with a smirk. "I'm guessing by that smile that he liked it. Didn't he?"

"Shut up." I punch him in the arm.

"Anyway, anything else I should know about?"

For a brief moment, I worry that he might find out the rest, but I just shake my head and change the subject. "Hey, would you and Nora like to meet him?"

"Didn't we already on Monday?"

"Well, not exactly, but I was thinking that today we could sit together, and you could get to know him."

"You really like this guy, don't you? I've never seen you hang out with someone as much as you've been hanging out with him."

His words hit strongly. I've been hanging out with Matthew so much that I might as well have been ignoring him and Nora. They can understand that. I'm still young and I'm enjoying the little moments I get with him. Those don't come very often, but with me, it seems like they do. "Yeah, I guess I do," I say. "But we can't keep hanging out so much without raising some alarms, mainly from my dad."

Alex gives me a smirk. "Ah, I see. You want to spend time with him here because it's safe."

"Yeah, and also introduce you guys to him."

"Well, I'd like to meet him. Let's do it."

The bell rings and we head towards homeroom. Not much happens except the occasional information of what's going to happen today. I send Matthew a message that Alex is in. I still need to talk to Nora but knowing her she'll want to meet him. Matthew sends me a smiling emoji along with a heart eyes emoji.

If I'm being honest, I feel good, as if riding on a wave of positivity. I think to myself, *Ok, maybe this can work. Maybe I can be with a boy and get a happy ending.* I'm still on thin ice with my parents, but all's well so far. If I can keep this hidden long enough to smooth them into my side, everything will be alright, but that can wait.

Let me first get through Nora and Alex meeting Matthew.

The introduction during lunch goes as planned. Matthew meets us in the courtyard after getting his lunch and Nora doesn't wait for him to sit down or take a bite of his food to start throwing questions at him. None of them are anything serious. She asks basic ones like where he's from and what he likes to do while keeping the more sensitive and more inappropriate questions to herself. She did try to get something personal out of him once, but he was smart. He smiled at her and then dodged it thoroughly. Nora saw right through it, but she seemed impressed at his reply because she decided not to bring it back up.

After a while, the conversation takes a turn. Nora stops acting like a detective and we move on to other things. We jump from topic to topic—as we usually do—and pass on words and advice on the subject of matter. Matthew took part of the conversation, speaking with confidence and security. I smile. Matthew trusts my friends, or, should I say, *our* friends. From what I can see, Nora and Alex have just welcomed Matthew into the gang.

The bell rings and we pick up our stuff and say goodbye for now, but we make a promise to plan to do something together on the weekend. When Nora and Alex are far enough, I turn to Matthew and say, "I think they liked you."

Matthew smiles. "It wasn't them I was trying to impress."

I blush at his compliment. When the bell rings, we say goodbye and head on to our classes. For the rest of the remaining periods, I feel happy, ecstatic. I'm light, glowing, butterflies flap inside my stomach. Things are going so well. I just wish I could introduce him to my parents. I know it's always weird, but I feel like that's an important step.

Too bad that'll never happen. My mom is still figuring her shit out, and my dad would freak when I mention the slightest thing about a romance with a boy.

My dad. I haven't thought about him for a while now. I've been so focused on Matthew that it hasn't come to mind. It feels nice, but I can't keep it aside. I still need to find a way to win him over. The whole "do what he wants so that he loves me" thing won't work forever. I need to set my ground, confront him, show him that I'm okay and that his rejection is what's hurting me.

Still one thing comes to mind, a question I can't answer with my optimism.

Can I win him over before everything blows up?

There's only one way to find out.

9

On my way home, I get a message from Nora.

> **Nora:** He's sooo cute!
> **Nora:** <<heart eyes emoji>> <<heart eyes emoji>> <<heart eyes emoji>>
> **Nora:** You sure know how to pick 'em.

I smile and start texting.

> **Me:** It was actually he who picked me.
> **Me:** He made the first move.
> **Nora:** Whatevs. He's still perfect for u.
> **Me:** In what way? <<raised eyebrow emoji>>
> **Nora:** In the "he makes you glow" kind of way.
> **Me:** Glow??? <<raised eyebrow emoji>>
> **Nora:** Yeah glow, shine, etc., etc. Who cares? What matters is that he definitely brightens things up in your life.
> **Me:** How, exactly?

Nora: <<sigh emoji>> I don't know. He's just does. Isn't that a core component of a relationship? Making the other happy for no reason.

Me: Well, I will admit, him being with me does make me happy.

Nora: Exactly.

Nora: Speaking of, how's operation get dad to see the light going?

Me: It's not going anywhere at all. Haven't even started on making a game plan. Been super busy.

Nora: On what???

Nora: Wait, have you been over Matthew's more than normal?

Me: No.

Nora: Liar. <<long nose emoji>>

I struggle with answering, but Nora sends another text before I can.

Nora: It's ok. You're falling in love. You're just enjoying the feeling. Once it sinks in, you'll be spending an appropriate amount of time together.

Nora: Just be careful, ok. Your dad definitely won't be happy if he finds out.

Me: Speaking of my dad, have you heard anything about him?

Nora: Not since his conversation with Kyle's dad. Still, be careful.

Nora: Gotta go. See u tomorrow.

I send her a goodbye text just as I turn onto my street. When I get home, the first thing I notice is that my dad's car isn't here, which brings me some relief. Mom on the other hand, is here. Her car being parked outside gives me all the information I need. When I walk through the door, I find her sitting in the living room, reading some book on her phone. I pass her by, and she gives me a smile. I smile back, then make my way towards the stairs.

Halfway up, I hear her voice. "Honey," she calls from the living room. "Could you come over here please?"

I don't know why, but my heartbeat rises. Maybe it's because we haven't had a private mother-to-son conversation since that moment up in my room. She hasn't brought it up any other time, and I didn't dare start the conversation myself. I was just giving her some space; letting her figure her stuff out so she can talk to me when she's ready. Maybe that's what she's doing now.

I go into the living room and stand a reasonable distance away from her. "Is something wrong?" I ask cautiously.

"No," she replies. "I just wanted to see how you were doing."

"Well, I'm doing great. So yeah."

"Good." A weak smile rests on her face. "Anything new happen?"

I can hear the worry in her voice. Maybe it's something else, but I feel like she's just trying to dance around the elephant in the room with these pointless questions. "No. Just the usual." A minute passes and neither she nor I say anything, so I decide to turn around and walk away.

"Wait," she says, her voice a little higher than usual. I turn around. She opens her mouth but says nothing. A part of her wants to say something. I see it in her eyes, but it's like she can't bring herself up to do it. I stand there for about thirty seconds before I say something.

"I really need to go so…"

Mom doesn't say anything, so I turn around and walk away.

I wait for her to call me back and to hear her say what she was going to say. When I get to the stairs, I stand there for a second waiting for her call. Nothing. I go up the stairs and on the second floor, I wait again. Same as before. I know she's probably not going to give it a shot. She was never that much of a risktaker.

When I walk into my room, I find myself feeling a bit down, but not because she didn't say anything. I'm over that already. It's how she looked at me. Before I came out, she would look at me like I was an open book. Ever since Saturday, it feels like she's missed a lot of what was between the lines. We used to talk about everything when I was younger, and she was open to anything. But now she's just—

Suddenly, I hear a knock come from my door. When I turn my head, I find myself surprised to see my mom, creeping her head in through the slightly open door. "You mind if I come in?" she asks.

I bite the inside of my lip, giving her a nod. She comes inside. She sits in my desk chair, and I take my bed. An awkward silence falls into the room.

"So…" I make my mouth into a giant O. "What's up?"

My mom doesn't say anything. Her eyes look down at the floor as if they were taking notice of the thousands of thin lines that are on each floorboard. Occasionally, she'd look back at me, then go back to looking at the floor. I didn't push her into getting to it. Starting this conversation is probably more difficult for her than it is for me. Finally, she closes her eyes, takes a deep breath, and begins. "I know that I'm a little late to start talking to you about this, but I just didn't know what I would even say."

I raise an eyebrow at her. She stops talking and avoids my line of sight again. She takes a deep breath and continues. "I know your father didn't take your news well, and I don't know what's going through your head right now, but I still love you. You know that, right?"

Does she know that her words don't matter if her actions don't speak the same thing? I don't say anything. She's trying, really trying, unlike dad, who's just angry and disappointed. He hasn't even brought up the topic since Saturday. I worry that if I bring it up, he might brush it off, scream at me, or worse. A beating maybe. I nod slightly, and she smiles.

"I know that I still have a ways to go," she continues, "but I'm hoping that you can help me along the way and so I was wondering if we could talk."

I'm... shocked! She wants to talk about this. She really wants to do this. I see it in her eyes. She's scared, a little bit, but she's here, asking for this conversation. She wants to know me, really know me. It makes me feel happy and scared. Nothing is scarier than opening up about your darkest secrets, especially to your own parents.

"Does dad know that you want to—"

"No," she cuts in. "He doesn't and it's probably for the best if he doesn't know for now. I don't know who he is right now, but for me to deal with this, I need to do it without him."

I smile. She's finally decided to take her own steps. She hasn't done that in so long. I'm happy for her. She's still afraid of dad. It's completely evident on her face, but she won't be in some time.

"Are you sure you're ready?" I ask her. I don't know why, but maybe I'm just being cautious. I don't want to get hurt.

My mom nods gently. Even still, I can see she's afraid. If I try to divert this, she might push her way to open up or maybe she'll leave it be. If it's the latter, I might have wasted a chance. Those don't come every day.

I take a deep breath and begin.

10

The way this works is that my mom asks me a question, and I give her an answer. Then she'll add something to what I said, and we'll tackle it for a while until we move on to the next question.

I'm surprised by the number of questions she has, but I'm more surprised by how they cover different subjects that I could consider sensitive, intrusive, or incredibly weird to discuss with my mother. Despite that, I answer them, but not without hesitating at first. When I finish talking, I lower my eyes and prepare myself for whatever she'll say. When she speaks, she never raises her voice or says something hurtful. Every single word is nice and encouraging, and it makes this conversation a little bit easier. It's still uncomfortable, but definitely a little easier.

"So, how long have you known?" she asks.

"A few years," I reply.

"Does anyone else know?"

"Just Nora and Alex." I thought about telling her that Matthew knows as well, but I'll do that when the time is right.

"How are you doing?"

A rather strange question, but I know where it's coming from. "I'm doing okay."

The conversation got a lot easier when my mom asked me if I've ever had a personal fantasy involving a boy. I didn't answer, but I could feel my cheeks turning red from embarrassment. She notices, bursts out laughing, and weirdly, I burst out laughing too. We get it out of our system for a while and when that's done, she tells me that it's perfectly normal for me to have fantasies like that and that it is nothing to be ashamed about. From then on, things go a lot smoother. We keep talking about other things, even those that are a big deal, and she's totally cool about it. She's careful with the way she words things, but it's still cool.

I wish dad were more like her. If he were, convincing him would be so much easier. I still need to figure out a way to get through to him, but the only person I know that was able to do that is my mom, and she hasn't done that in so long. He's been getting more stubborn about his control, and he's not even letting her have any power in family decisions. I find it weird that she hasn't asked for a divorce. If I were her, I would've left and never come back, and I would especially take me out of his reach. I doubt I'd survive living alone with him, especially now that I've came out.

We keep talking, sharing, and laughing for longer than I expected. By the time the conversation ends, the sun had already set, and a smile is resting on my mother's face. I smile too. It's nice to not worry about myself after the last few days. Wish I could say this could last longer.

"How 'bout you and I go have dinner at the diner on Main Street?" my mom says.

I raise an eyebrow. "Really? What about dad?"

"He's working late, and he won't be back until late at night. So, it's just you and me. What do you say?"

My smile widens. "Why not."

We get to the diner in just under thirty minutes, and they seat us on a booth in the corner that gives us a full view of the place. We order our usuals: burgers and fries with diet cokes. I order myself a milkshake as well. When it all gets here, we start eating and I eclearn my plate within five minutes. It's a habit of mine to eat quickly, as if they're going to take the food away from me. It's not like there's a problem with eating quickly. It's just that it leaves me wanting more, and I will over-eat if I eat more, leaving me with stomach pain.

When I finish eating, I wipe my mouth with a nap-kin and set the plate aside. It's a custom of mine to have the plate ready for the waiter to take it. Mom's plate still has some food left on it: half of the burger and a couple of fries. She notices me eying her food, and smiles. "You want some?" she asks.

I shake my head. "No thanks. I've had enough." I notice her watching me curiously. "What is it?"

Mom takes another bite of her burger. "Nothing. It just feels nice to see you happy again."

"*Happy* again?" I raise an eyebrow.

"Yeah. Ever since you came out to us, I've been see-ing you with this worried face, as if you were afraid that something was going to happen." She tilts her head. "Is it because of your father? If it is, don't worry."

For a moment, I hadn't been thinking about him, but now, I remember everything that's going on with him: his anger, his disapproval, his thought of sending me to conversion therapy. I think of the last one the most. Alex and Nora haven't heard anything, and from what I've seen in the house it doesn't look like he's researching it. I could be wrong. He could be keeping it all a secret. It could all be in his office or on his computer, places that I don't have access to.

Does mom know about this? Does she know what dad thinks about me? "Did you know that dad was asking Mr. Bartow for information about the conversion clinic where Kyle is?"

My mom's expression changes. That says it all. "I was really hoping he wouldn't do that," she says.

"So, you knew?" I try to sound as calm as possible.

She nods slightly. "He mentioned it the night you came out. I tried to talk some sense into him, and we argued about it, but it looks like it didn't make that much of a difference."

For a minute none of us say anything. Then she says, "I'm not going to let him send you away."

I raise my head. "How, exactly?"

She puts a hand on my shoulder. "I don't know, but I won't let him do that. You leave me to deal with your father. If he's going to send you away, he'll have to go through me first. I promise."

I smile at her, and though I feel like I'm about to cry, I lay my head on her shoulder and hold her tightly.

11

I welcome the final bell after a nightmarish class discussion about the anatomy of the human leg. Who knew that there were so many components that contributed to a single body part? Thankfully, the class came to an end and there's no school tomorrow, so I have three full days to recharge.

When the teacher dismisses us, I walk out of the classroom and head towards my locker where I put away my books. After that, I make my way out of school. Not even ten steps after I walk off school grounds, I hear a familiar voice call my name. I turn around to see Matthew running towards me. "Mind if I join you?" he asks.

I smile. "Sure. Hope you're wearing comfy shoes."

Matthew laughs and we get to walking. Normally,

the route I take to go home goes through the suburbs and gets me home in like thirty minutes. Today on the other hand, I go take the longest way possible, which in this case goes through the heart of town at a simple and slow pace, which is not how I normally walk. I'm always walking as if I have to be somewhere immediately. Today, on the other hand, it's different. Matthew is with me, and he makes me feel like I'm in less of a hurry.

As we cross Main Street, Matthew and I don't say much. We'd occasionally turn to look at each other and smile, but we don't exchange a single word or glance or signs. We walk side by side at a good distance, but even still, I feel like grabbing his hand. I hold back the urge. Anyone could see us, and if it's someone who's close with my dad, Matthew will be out in the open, even if I come up with the greatest lie possible. This town is full of people who'd fall prey to anything. When it comes to the words of others, my dad would be a victim to everyone's misunderstandings and lies.

I keep my hands buried in my pockets, occasionally playing with whatever few dollars and cents that I have in them. Yet for some weird reason, my palms feel a little warmer than usual, almost as if Matthew is holding them. The thought of that brings me back to his room when he pressed his lips to mine and when we lay down on his bed. I get lost in the memory for a while before Matthew drags me out by saving me from crashing into a pole. "You okay?" he asks.

I nod at him, but I'm honestly not sure.

We haven't spoken about that since yesterday, and he hasn't tried to bring it up or do anything else. The whole thing makes me feel like he's pretending that it never happened. But it did happen, and we both liked it. Why hasn't he tried anything else or even bothered to talk about it? I'm not expecting another hookup or something like that, but I would at least like it if he and I could spend some time together somewhere. Not that it would even be possible. We could never go out anywhere without being seen.

But still...

"So, how've you been?" Matthew asks me.

I look at him. "Pretty good, honestly," I reply. A minute of silence. I don't know what else to say. But I'm wondering if I should bring up the topic of our encounter or wait for later.

"Say, do you know anything about the bonfire party that everybody's talking about?"

Wait for later it is. "Yeah. It's scheduled to happen two weeks from Saturday."

"I already know that, but I'm curious to know if you're going."

I raise an eyebrow. "Are you asking me if I want to go with you?"

Matthew doesn't look shocked. He raises his shoulders and in a calm tone, he says, "I guess I am. Do you wanna go?"

I don't answer. My mind is spinning around with how he wants me to go to that party with him. Truth be told, I want to say yes. I want to go with him, dance with him, have fun regardless of who may see. Still, that's the part that worries me. If I go with him, I'll be outing myself to the whole class, who'll then talk about the whole thing, then their parents might get wind of it and then they'll tell mine and then I'll be in trouble with dad. Gossip spreads like wildfire and it never misses anyone.

But it's more than that. I feel like I barely know him. The last time we really got to know each other was back in my room when we passed each other little details about ourselves. Apart from that, after our encounter, I'm not sure what we are. We certainly aren't boyfriends. That word doesn't fit with what we are. I don't even think that there's a word that can define this thing between us, which makes describing this really, *really* hard, and confusing.

Matthew puts a hand on my shoulder. "Hey, it's okay if you don't want to go. I know that you still don't want anyone to know. I can tell by your face, so if you like, we can—"

"No," I jump in. Matthew pulls his hand away as I continue. "I want to go, but you're right. I still don't want anyone to know, and that's not all."

I stop speaking. Somehow, it feels like my tongue got tied up. "You and I... I don't exactly know what you and I are, but I feel like we have something. It's just that we haven't done anything since that day at your house. We haven't spoken about making any other steps and I feel like we've just been standing still. You want me to go to a dance with you, and that's fine, but I feel like we still don't know each other well. So how I can I say yes?"

Matthew takes in what I've just said. His eyes look lost and shocked, which tends to make me panic a bit. Finally, he replies. "So, you don't want to come because you feel like you barely know me?"

The tone of his voice frightens me. Sweat fills up my palms. "Sort of. I like you. I really do, but I feel like we're jumping a few important steps. Can we just go on a date first, please? From there, we could try and get to know each other a little better and then see where this goes."

Matthew scratches the back of his head. A part of me worries that I might've just blown this whole thing up. "Alright," he says. "We can go on a first date. What would you like to do?"

I smile and then shake my head. "What would *you* like to do? It was my idea to do this so how 'bout you tell me what you want to do, and I'll make it happen."

Matthew gives me a perfect smile. His eyes sparkle and a part of me wishes I could kiss him right about now. He leans closer to me and whispers, "I want you to surprise me," into my ear.

I nod at him when he moves back and as we come out of Main Street, I take a risk and grab his hand.

Matthew and I keep walking until we get to my house. Once we're there, he gives me a goodbye hug and I walk inside.

"Mom," I call out. Her car is parked outside, but

she doesn't respond. Still, an all too familiar voice does. "Taylor," my dad calls out coldly. "Could you come up here for a second?"

At the sound of his voice, my stomach twists into a knot, but I proceed to go upstairs to my parents' bedroom. Dad's in there, sitting on his desk chair working through a few papers. He's taken his suit jacket off, leaving only his white-collar shirt and semi loosened tie on. I come into the room and his attention is immediately driven towards me. "Is something wrong?" I ask.

My dad sets the papers on his hand down and replies. "No. I was just wondering how you're doing."

My first thought is to ask him why he cares, and my second thought is to say how he thinks I feel. I bite my tongue. The thin ice tension that our relationship has is still here, slowing trying to regain its strength. He's still angry with me, but not as angry as he was on Saturday. It's been cooling off bit by bit, but I can still feel his anger and disappointment.

"I'm good," I tell him. A minute of silence.

My dad takes off his glasses and says, "So I hear you've been getting along with Matthew?"

I nod gently, but I know better. He's not pulling these questions just because he's heard about it. He's asking because he probably saw us hugging through the window. I shouldn't have done that. *Idiot*, I tell myself. "He's a really nice guy. We've been hanging out a lot."

"And I heard that you two hung out after school on Monday," he says. "Where did you two go?"

The tension is growing. He knows where I went. He's just asking out of the hope that I'll crack and tell him everything. He thinks I'm an idiot but when it comes to reading a family member, I learned from the best: him. It's a good thing nobody saw us holding hands, because if he knows about that, he'll send me away, even if nothing more happened that day. I saw the brochure of the conversion clinic among his things. He still has it in mind, but I hope only as a last precaution.

"We only went over to the bookstore," I say. "He wanted to find a book and I accompanied him."

"Why?" he asks.

"Just so we can talk a bit and keep getting along. We really hit it off on Sunday and he was busy during lunch."

My dad eyes me sternly. Somewhere in my head, I hear a voice telling me that this is where it all ends. Another voice tells me to keep calm, and that he won't find anything, and that mom will protect me. But she's not here right now, so he can do what he wants without worry, as long as it doesn't leave any evidence. I silently pray that he just drops this, or that something unexpectedly comes up that I could use it as a reason to get out of here.

Like an answer from God, my phone dings, and I excuse myself to get out of the room. As I walk through the door frame, my dad surprises me by speaking. "Don't get too friendly with him," he says. I don't say anything or nod. I just go to my room.

Once I'm there, I exhale in relief. That was a close one. If I stayed there any longer, I might've cracked. What he said to me last was definitely a warning. He'll be keeping an eye on me whenever I'm around, but it won't be that much. He's not paranoid enough to start following me around as if he were a spy. Still, when I'm around him in the house, he'll be watching me.

I should probably tell Matthew that the date has to be called off. It's probably for the best. I need to wait for this to die down. Then again, I don't think I'll ever get another chance and Matthew is already excited to go out with me for the first time. *Think, Taylor*, I tell myself.

An idea comes to mind. I pull out my phone and text Nora.

> **Me:** Hey. Need ur help??
> **Nora:** What is it?
> **Me:** Matthew and I wanna go on a date and we need an alibi, so can you and Alex be our separate alibis?
> **Nora:** Sure thing. Name the time and place and we'll be ready.
> **Me:** I was thinking tomorrow since I have the day to plan.
> **Me:** Btw, my dad's getting on my radar.
> **Nora:** What happened?
> **Me:** He's getting suspicious about my friendship with Matthew, and he's already warned me to not try anything.
> **Nora:** Damn! <<mind blown emoji>> Did he get anything out of you?
> **Me:** No, and I hope he doesn't. That's what I need the alibi for. It'll make it impossible for him to put us together when this happens.
> **Nora:** Alright, so what are you planning?
> **Me:** Not sure. Still trying to figure it out.
> **Me:** He asked for me to surprise him, but I don't know what to do.
> **Nora:** Got any ideas?
> **Me:** I was thinking of doing a movie, but we can't go out late and we can't do it at the theatre, my house, or his.
> **Nora:** Then do it in mine. My parents will

be out all day at work, so I pretty much
have the house to myself. You can use the
basement.

Me: You'd do that for me?

Nora: <<thumbs up emoji>> <<thumbs up
emoji>> <<thumbs up emoji>>

Me: Ok. Do you have any movies that we
could use?

Nora: Of course, I do. Come here tomorrow
and pick one out.

I send Nora a thumbs up emoji and I set the phone down. For the next ten minutes, I think of a couple of details before texting Alex to loop him in. I tell him that I need him to be Matthew's alibi and also pick him up since he's the only one of us who has a car. I tell him that all he has to do is lie about where he and Matthew are going and then come over to Nora's when he starts asking about the date.

Alex: What exactly is your plan for your
date?

Me: A movie. Nora offered us her basement.

Alex: Ok. What about me and Nora? What
do we do?

Me: Whatever you want. As long as you stay
upstairs.

Alex: Aww man! <<winning emoji>> I really
want to see how you make a move.

Me: My love life is not a show to see. It's a

life, so let me play it out with zero worries.
Alex: <<sigh emoji>> Fine but tell me about it later. See u tomorrow.

I say goodbye to Alex and write to Matthew.
Me: Hey, I got the whole date planned for tomorrow.
Matthew: Wow. That was fast. So, what are we doing?
Me: You told me to surprise you so I'm going to surprise you. Alex will pick you up and take you to Nora's house in the afternoon.
Matthew: <<smiling emoji>> I'm already excited. Anything I should do?
Me: Just be yourself, and dress in something nice but still casual. We're not heading somewhere fancy or anywhere at all.
Matthew: <<thumbs up emoji>> You got it!

I smile.

12

With there being no school Friday, I pretty much have the whole morning to get things ready for the date.

First comes a shower and then brushing my teeth. After that, I get dressed, grab a quick breakfast and head out the door. I tell my mom that I'll be hanging out with Nora for a while and split before she can ask me about it. Even though she's cool with me being gay, I feel that telling her about Matthew is probably not a good idea, at least not yet. I'll tell her about him alright, but it's going to be a while, probably when dad's been sort of taken care of.

I walk over to Nora's. She doesn't live that far from me, so I get to her house in like fifteen minutes without sweating like a pig. Thank goodness for the breeze. As soon as I reach her front door, I ring the doorbell and am immediately greeted by a tight hug from her. She's dressed in a pair of white denim shorts and a blue crop top. Her hair is pulled back in a messy ponytail. "You look like you're dressed to impress," she says.

I look down at my outfit, a simple plain t-shirt with jeans and sneakers. "I don't see it," I tell Nora.

She rolls her eyes. "Wow. You really need help. Anyway, come on." She grabs my hand and pulls me in.

We head down to the basement. There isn't much down there except for a couch, a TV, a coffee table, and a pool table that Nora's dad got last year. Normally on a chill day like this, me, Nora, and Alex would hang in here and watch something on TV, talk, and maybe play pool. The last one won't be the most obvious since Nora would always beat our asses because of how much time she spends with the table. She also happens to be super competitive, going so far as keeping track of all the time she's beaten me and Alex; seventy-eight in total, if I count right.

I get a text from Matthew saying that Alex has already picked him up. He'll be here in thirty minutes, which gives me enough time to get everything ready.

We waste no time. Nora and I tidy the place up a bit but, thankfully, there isn't much work to be done because Nora's housekeeper came by yesterday. After that, I set up some snacks from a stash Nora keeps hidden while Nora cooks up a frozen pizza. I hope Matthew likes pepperoni. While she waits for it to finish, I stay in the basement scrounging through the movies she has. It's actually a little bit complicated because most of the movies Nora has to offer are action, drama or historical, which may be typical for her, but I don't feel like they fit into the moment right now. Maybe I should've brought a film of my own.

I bring this up to Nora when she comes back. Luckily, she has a backup plan. "There's a couple of Hallmark movies recorded on the cable box," she says. "Feel free to scroll through them and see what you like."

I nod at her and get scrolling. She has roughly twelve movies to choose from, and all of them are practically following the same "boy meets girl, boy loses girl, boy gets girl" theme. The only difference between them is the storyline. Nora made us watch them with her sometimes and though it was fun at first, watching different movies that are almost the same is really tiresome. Can't they spice up the story a little bit, maybe add something intense or whatnot?

I settle for a simple drama movie released a few

years back. It's one of my all-time favorites and to be honest, the narrative is really good, as is the lesson and the romance. I think Matthew would like it. Once that's settled, I do a last-minute check of everything. When everything is ready to go, I sit down and wait.

"Are you nervous?" Nora asks me.

I nod at her. "A little."

"You wanna go through what you plan to say to him?"

I shake my head. "Nah, I'm good. I think I'll just go with the flow."

She pats me on the back. "You're gonna be fine."

I raise an eyebrow. "How do you know?"

Nora smiles. "Because I believe in you."

When the doorbell rings, I immediately rise. I make my way up the stairs and to the door and stop. I breathe in deeply, place a hand on the knob and twist it open.

Matthew is right in front of me, dressed in a pair of jeans with a yellow tie dye shirt under an open green flannel shirt. His blonde hair is all curled up, and a couple pieces cover a bit of his forehead. In one hand, he holds a couple of flowers. Nothing too romantic, just a few wildflowers that I noticed growing out in his front yard. Still, the gesture is pretty nice.

I pull him by the shirt and kiss him as the door closes behind us. He kisses me back, gently at first, then a little bit stronger. My hands run all over his back, and he pulls me in tighter. The flowers in his hand get crushed by our conjoined chests. Regardless, we keep kissing.

We separate after a minute, and I stare into his eyes. "Hi," I say.

"Hey," he says. We're still close to one another. He lifts up the partially crushed wildflowers up to me and says, "For you."

I take the flowers into my hands. Some of them, if not all, are already broken with petals doomed to fall soon, but they still look good. "Thank you," I say to him.

Matthew smiles. For a moment, I feel like we're going to kiss again, but the front door opens and Alex waltzes in. He looks at us, and when he sees the rose in my hand and Matthew's arm wrapped around me, he says, "Save the romance for your date." A small laugh escapes me.

"Where's Nora?" Alex asks.

"She's downstairs," I say. By now, Matthew has let me go. "Remember, you and Nora stay up here and keep guard."

"Alright," Alex says. "You guys have fun."

Alex walks down in search of Nora. I turn to Matthew. "You ready?" I ask him.

Matthew smiles. "Whenever you are," he replies.

I smile at him and plant a kiss on his lips.

So, here's what happens.

Nora and Alex go upstairs, but they would occasionally creep downstairs on their own to peek at us. After a few times of spotting them and one confrontation between them, they leave us be.

As for Matthew and me, things pretty much go smoothly. We play the movie and chow down on the available snacks and pizza slices as we do so. We talk throughout the movie, but the words get lost through the dialogue and sounds. Our focus is less on the movie and more on each other. Something about him makes me want to watch him a little longer, and maybe I long to be closer to him than I am. We're already so close to one another, and I can feel his body heat radiating. It takes me like a storm.

The movie is almost over when Matthew places his hand on my knee. It feels so heavy, but also light. I take his hand into mine as the movie comes to an end. As the credits roll, he looks at me and smiles. "I love you," he says.

I freeze. My nerves shock and I immediately start to panic. Did he just say that he loves me? He definitely did. I heard him right. My heartbeat rises. Sparks light up within me and a breath escapes my lips.

Matthew's still looking at me. His hand is still in mine. At this moment, he looks different to me, more vibrant than ever. A smile rests on his face, but his eyes tell a different story. He's worried about me. I haven't said anything back. "Was it too much?" he asks.

For some reason, I answer as if I was under pressure. "Well, I…" My voice falters. I don't know what to say. I don't expect to say something perfect, but I want this to at least be meaningful. Do I say I love you back? I think I should but not out of the bloom, not when it may be interpreted as if I'm saying what he wants to hear.

"It's okay," Matthew says. He takes his hand back. "I don't know what's going through your head, but I—"

"No," I reply back. Matthew stops talking. I straighten myself up and continue. "It wasn't a lot. It's just that… I don't know. Don't you think it's too soon?"

"Maybe." He leans in a little closer. "But a part of

me feels like I've known you longer than I really do. I know it may sound strange, but… you complete me. I really, *really* love you."

He said it again: *I love you*. Butterflies flap in my stomach. I smile at him and say, "I feel the same way, but I'm worried. If my dad catches us, who knows what he'll do. And who knows what your parents Matthew do to you."

Matthew leans into me. "I rather not think about that. It'll definitely kill the good vibes we have between us. Besides, we'll be careful. We can keep meeting like this, and Nora and Alex can help us."

"Are you sure they're up for that?" I ask.

"They already appear to be in on it from what I see. We can do this."

He sounds… hopeful, as if our story is going to end like a book or a movie. I believe we can get that ending as well. Maybe or maybe not. There are so many risks to this, and despite him being able to feel confident and hopeful, I can't share the same feeling. *I'm sorry,* I want to tell him, *I bear the weight of the trouble so you can remain as you are.* Maybe someday I'll be able to walk with him without any worries going through me, but for now, I'm treading on dangerous ground.

"You're still worried, aren't you," Matthew says.

I nod. "I can't help it. If they catch us—"

"We'll be careful," Matthew breaks in. He leans in a little more. I can feel his breath hit my face. "We can game plan our next steps later, but I need to know if you're in or not."

I look into his eyes and feel as if they're saying, *Please, let him say yes.* I want to, I really do, but if we're caught, it'll all be over. We'll never see each other again, and God only knows what'll come next for us. But if I say no, this might be over anyway, only it'll end today, at this moment. He'll probably end it and back away. I don't want that.

But...

"I'm scared," I tell him.

"I know," he whispers to me. "I'm scared as well, but we deserve our own love story as much as anyone else." He takes a hold of my hand. "Maybe, if we were together, I'd have your back and you'd have mine. Maybe then, we wouldn't be so scared."

His words sound like a promise, as if he were telling me that he'll be there for me. I believe them, and I believe him. He seems to notice my reaction because he smiles. "So, I guess this means you're in," he says.

I smile and plant a kiss on his lips. It's a quick kiss, but it's enough to make his smile widen. As I move away from him, I say, "Does that answer your question?"

Matthew blushes. We kiss again, only this time, with Nora and Alex watching from behind the corner.

13

The next two weeks are like a fairy tale.

Matthew and I keep hanging out discreetly. Sometimes, we use Nora and Alex as a cover for us when we're out in the streets or at their houses. In public, we keep our hands and lips to ourselves. Privately, on the other hand, we're free to touch and kiss, but with the occasional problem that they're with us. When we want to be alone, we go hang out at Matthew's place, which thankfully, is always empty since his parents are always out working, giving us the perfect spot to let our guards down.

Thanks to his house being far from everybody, we have the freedom Matthew talked about when I first went there. We can hold hands, kiss, squeeze in together in ways that we can't do in public out of fear of being spotted. We could talk about anything as if we were sitting in front of one another in a restaurant. Our conversations—both meaningful and meaningless—make the time pass so quickly that he has to always pressure me into going home. Thankfully, Matthew has a solution for all the ground I need to cover. Fun fact: Matthew's dad has a motorcycle in his garage, and Matthew happens to know how to ride it. When he told me that he knew how to ride the damn thing, I pictured him in a leather jacket, fingerless gloves, a wallet chain, and some cool ass shades.

With the idea of him dressed like that, I could only describe him with one word: *Hot.*

I actually shared this image of him one day when we were cuddled up in his bed. Once I tell him that, I share a little fantasy I had of us riding like crazy to who knows where. When I finished, Matthew smiled, and said, "Well how 'bout we one day take a trip together like that?"

I crack up a little bit, but when I realize that he's serious about it, I stop myself. "Would your parents allow you to do that?"

Matthew scratches the back of his head. "Well, not exactly," he says. "They don't let me ride it and they don't know that I've used it before. I just borrow it without them knowing and take it for a spin on my own. So that's what we'll be doing."

"Well, you do know that we can't do that, unless you want to get caught and have either of our parents connect the dots."

"I wasn't talking about riding around town for the heck of it. I was thinking about us going on a trip together. Someday, when we graduate or in the summer, we can pack our bags and get the hell out of here. Maybe we could go somewhere far away. Just the two of us."

I raise an eyebrow. "Are you suggesting we do that, just take off together?"

Matthew leans closer to me. "Only if you want to."

I scooch over to him. "Where would we even go?"

"Wherever you want," he replies.

I smile and rest my head on his shoulder. Matthew raises a hand and begins stroking my hair. His fingers spread out to cover more of my scalp. When they retreat, they massage it with the tips of the nails. It feels nice, all of it.

Something about all these times when we're together makes me think of the future. I picture us doing what Matthew suggested. We get on a bike and just ride off to someplace for an adventure or for freedom. He'll be the one driving the thing. I'll be sitting behind him with my arms wrapped around his belly. He also won't be wearing a helmet so when the wind blows his hair back, some—if not all of it—touches my face.

I picture other things, going way further. I picture us graduating, going to college together, getting married, having kids, and watching them grow. Then, once the kids are all grown up, we ride around in an RV and go state by state making good memories until we decide to spend our last years together in a beach house somewhere down in who knows where. Florida maybe. This all sounds silly, and I know it. Still, I can't help myself. He's everything I want in life. Is it bad if I imagine our future together so soon?

A part of me says that I shouldn't think of these things. I feel like a day will come that I'm going to lose him somehow. Maybe it's because of my dad. Despite the days passing by, my dad is still angry and though we've been careful to avoid any suspicion, and that he hasn't hit me again or anything, the tension is still there. I feel like a day will come where he would just go ahead with his idea about conversion therapy and send me away.

Mom keeps telling me that she's handling it, and even though I don't see it, I can tell that she's trying. Sometimes, I'd walk in a room and see them looking at each other as if they had an argument and were angry with one another. Other times, I could hear the conversations all the way downstairs while I was in my room. It doesn't matter whether I can hear the arguments or not. Either way, dad is not changing his opinion about it.

I keep informing Matthew about my situation at home. He does the same with his, but mine are more serious than his. I rant like crazy about it, and at one point, I stopped myself after I realized that I didn't take into consideration how this might affect him. His parents don't know anything, and he thinks that it's for the best. After what happened with my parents, I'd most definitely agree, but with what's happening with my mom, I feel like maybe he should come out.

We talked about it one day. We were out in his backyard having a little homemade picnic when I brought the topic about him coming out to his parents again. After a bit of talking, I asked, "Do you at least think that they can change?"

Matthew turns his head to me. "Maybe," he says

weakly.

I take in his response. "You don't think that they can. Do you?"

Matthew lowers his head. "I'm not sure. They don't seem to strike me as the ones who can accept something that goes against their beliefs. That's why I always pictured taking off as soon as I'm old enough and never looking back. I figured that when I do that, I would be free from my dad's control and can become whoever I want to be."

"Where would you go?"

Matthew looks at me. "Wherever it is that I feel like I belong. That's what we all have to do: leave home to find ourselves. I always figured that when I graduate, I would close the past and start a new life. Then I met you and I felt as if all this time, I was just being kept where I was so that I could meet you."

I smile and lean a little closer to him. "The day before I met you, I felt as if I had gotten myself into hot water. I told my parents the truth and our relationship changed as a whole. Then the very next day, I saw you and a part of me felt that you were my ticket out. When you told me that we could escape, I believed that, and I believed that you could help me out."

Matthew strokes my cheek with his hand. "Have I helped you like you expected?"

I nod. "You're doing it right now."

Matthew smiles and plants a kiss on my lips. "Do you want me to take you out?"

I raise an eyebrow. "Out? As in a date?"

Matthew nods.

"Well, I'd love that, but where would we go?"

"You let me figure that out, but now, I need to know if you want to."

I smile and lean into him until my head is on his shoulder. "Yes, I do," I whisper into his ear.

Matthew hugs and whispers two things into my ear: one, I have to wait for him to plan everything.

And two, we'll be getting out of our comfort zone.

In the days that followed, I continued to ask myself what exactly he meant by getting out of our comfort zone.

Matthew gave me a brief description. "We're going somewhere where we can be out in the open," he said, and he doesn't give any more details than that, which makes this super confusing to me. It's not like there isn't a queer scene in this town. We do have one, but not a very strong one, and whoever is part of it has to deal with all the homophobes and bigots that come here. That's how Kyle got in trouble with his parents. Someone spotted him walking into a queer support group meeting, and after being confronted about it, he confessed and was sent off to a conversion clinic. Since I know Matthew is smart enough to not take any risks, he most likely is picking something different.

I think of possible places that he might go. When I take out places that are romantic and public such as restaurants and parks, there's only a few places he could choose from. The options he has are either the lakes, the stores that we can visit and be hidden, like the book-store, and the hiking trails.

Maybe he's planning on taking me out for a hike. There's a lot of trails around town and I wouldn't be surprised if his idea of a date would be a walk in the woods. It's not that bad of an idea at all. We could walk, take in the fresh air, maybe even swim in one of the lakes or streams that are hidden. There's also a few caves deep in the woods, which would be good for us to spend some time alone.

Thinking of this makes me think of how fast things have flown between us. From total strangers to start dating, it feels like a few months spanned in a few weeks. A relationship born from day one. We still don't call it a relationship, the same way we don't call ourselves boyfriends just yet. But we're getting there.

It's just a matter of time.

I talk to Matthew about it in the hope of being ready. Apparently, Matthew says that I guessed wrong and when I ask him what he's planning, he insists on keeping it a surprise for me.

"Well, can you at least tell me *when* and *where* it's going to happen?" I ask him.

Matthew sighs, but he replies. "Saturday night and it's in the city."

I raise an eyebrow. "In Baltimore?"

Matthew nods.

"Okay. Wait, Saturday night. That's the date the bonfire party is scheduled for."

Matthew nods. "It gives us the perfect cover we need to sneak out."

I wanted to ask him about where we're sneaking to, but Matthew ends it there by walking away. It was only as I got home that I get a message from him with some instructions on what to do. The last text is a question.

Matthew: Do you feel ready to get out of
  your comfort zone?

I smile.

Me: Yes.

And just like that, everything is set up.

14

"You ready Taylor?" Nora calls from downstairs.

I slip my head through my door. "In a minute," I yell back.

Tonight's the night. Matthew and I are sneaking out of the bonfire party to go wherever it is that he's planning on taking us. He said that he'll send me a message when he gets there and until then, I should have some fun while I'm there. With him not telling me where we're going, I've been anxiously waiting for this night. Now that it's here, my excitement is through the roof.

As the night settled in, I scrounged through my closet in search something to wear. In this case, I choose a simple white t-shirt with blue denim shorts and sneakers. After that, I scrubbed myself hard on the shower, brushed my teeth, and combed my hair until there wasn't a single strand out of place. I put my clothes on and go into my parent's room in search of my dad's cologne. He always had a good taste, and I will admit, the scents he picks are intoxicating. I grab the one he uses when he goes out with mom and spray some on me. Finding it wasn't that hard since it's got a tape marking it and he also left out in the open when he went out with mom an hour ago.

It's a good thing that neither of my parents are here. If they were, they'd both be asking questions as to why I'm putting an effort to look so good. I may have been keeping my relationship with Matthew a secret, but they're not stupid. Both would notice the cologne and immediately think that I'm trying to make an effort to impress someone. I don't want to lie to my parents, especially my mom, but I really need to keep this hidden for now.

Once I'm ready, I head downstairs where I find Nora and Alex waiting for me in the living room. Nora is wearing a plain white dress with a pair of brown sandals that show off her red painted toenails. Alex has a white cotton shirt on with a pair of beige colored cargo shorts and sneakers. The bonfire party is a white party so everyone will be wearing something white. When I come into the room, both turn their attention to me. Nora inhales a bit, then looks me in the eye. "Are you wearing some of your dad's cologne?" she asks.

"How do you even know that it's my dad's?" I ask.

"Taylor, I know because you don't have any. So, are you planning on asking Matthew to dance or something?"

I smile. "Actually, Matthew is taking me out on a little adventure."

Nora rests her chin on the palm of her hand. "Really? Where's he taking you?"

I raise my shoulders. "Beats me. He's planning on surprising me, but I'm still very excited."

She rolls her eyes. "What is it with you two and surprises?" She groans, and I can't help but laugh a bit.

Alex doesn't say a word. "Is something wrong?" I ask him.

Alex looks up at me. "Nothing. I'm just curious, do you know how long you're going to be gone?"

I shake my head. "I'm not sure. He says that we're going out of town, so I don't really know where we're going."

Nora adds. "Well, if anything happens, we'll cover

for you guys. We'll tell your parents that you guys are staying with us or something. That way, they won't get suspicious."

I smile at her. "Where would I be without you guys?"

"Probably in some miserable hellhole that you got yourself into."

I laugh. "Oh, that's cruel."

"You still love me either way."

"True."

"Say," Alex says, "is there any special reason for why you're going out like this? You guys have been hanging out in secret for two weeks. What's with the sudden change?"

I place my hands behind me and explain to them everything. I tell them about the motorcycle, my fantasy, our talk and how we ended up making plans to do this little trip of ours out of town. When I finish, Nora looks at me and says, "You really, really like him, don't you?"

I smile. "Well, now it's less 'I like him' and more 'I love him.'"

"But have you told him that?" she asks.

My smile fades. Have I told him that I love him already? Now that I think about it, I haven't, at all. I never even said it back to him at Nora's basement. Somewhere I got lost that it just slipped out of my head. Not even in the two weeks that I was hanging out with him have I said the words to his face. I have thought about it, moments when I thought, *God, I love him* as we cuddled in his bed or lay on the grass in his backyard, but I never thought about telling him that.

Nora's eyes widen. "You haven't told him yet, have you?"

I don't bother denying it. "No."

"Why?"

I scratch the back of my head. "Because, I haven't found the right time."

Nora gets up and grabs my hand. "I'm gonna say this to you because I care about you. You've got to tell him tonight. If not tonight, then sometime later, but it has to be soon. Trust me on this: those three words hold a lot of power."

Her words frighten me a bit. I get what she means by that. I felt the power of those words when Matthew said them to me, and I can tell that he's been waiting for me to say them. "I'll make sure to tell him tonight. I promise."

Nora smiles then looks at her watch. "Okay," she says, "much as I'd like to know how you'll express your love to Matthew, we need to get going. The party must've started by now."

Alex and I nod at her, and we head out.

If there's one good thing that the bonfire party brings into my plan to slip out of here is that the only light source is the bonfire itself. When I need to sneak out, no one will see me disappear into the darkness.

When we reach the party, the fire is already burning at its strongest. Dozens of wooden boards, logs, and sticks are packed together and transformed into dust by the flames. More wood is set beside it, waiting for its turn to burn. All around the fire are groups of two or more, dancing, singing, and swinging. The flames light up one or two parts of them, casting shadows on the park's grass. To a side lies a DJ set with a Top 100 song blasting out of the speakers. The scent of burned wood and wildlife fills the air.

As soon as we're close to the bonfire, Nora and Alex pull me in to dance. I try my best to resist them. I feel like waiting for Matthew to send me a message. "Come on," Nora whines. "I'm sure you can spare a few seconds to dance. Besides, you like this song." I sigh and move in to join them.

Nora leads me and Alex. She starts to dance between us while Alex dances in front of her. I dance in the back. My movements are simple. I'm not much of a dancer. As for Nora and Alex, their movements were more progressive, as if they knew how to dance together.

Which to be honest, they do.

I've always felt like they liked each other. I don't know why, but I felt that it was written based on how they looked at each other. Alex always looked at Nora in a way, like if she were special or something. Nora seemed to blush when she saw Alex sometimes. I don't know why they haven't yet gone forward with it. Who knows? Maybe they just don't want to risk ruining their friendship.

At that point, my phone dings. It's Matthew.

Matthew: I'm out by the parking lot.
Me: 'Kay. Headin' there now. <<heart eyes emoji>>

I turn to Nora and Alex. "Matthew's here," I tell them.

Nora leans in and gives me a brief hug. "Alright. I'll text you in case something happens."

"Have fun," Alex says.

I nod at them and head off. Sneaking out undetected is easy when everyone's too busy having fun to notice someone leaving so soon. It gets a lot easier when I get further away from the bonfire flames. The sound of the music dissipates as I walk, and so does the other kid's voices and the bonfire light. Once I'm in the parking lot, it's all far behind me.

I spot Matthew standing under a streetlight, and when he comes into clear view, my eyes widen. He's dressed in a pair of tattered black jeans with a black jacket over a dark red t-shirt. His blonde hair is covered by a black cap and his hands are covered by a pair of riding gloves. Next to him lies his dad's motorcycle. It's charcoal black paint job reflects the light from the street.

A breath escapes me as I approach him. "You look… *hot.*"

Matthew laughs. "Is that the best you got?"

"Well, I wasn't expecting…" I gesture to his outfit. "This."

Matthew looks at his clothes. "If I'm gonna be riding a motorcycle with the guy I love, I might as well dress like a badass. What do you think?"

I smile and give him a kiss. "You look awesome," I whisper into his ear.

Matthew leans into my ear. "And you look beautiful."

My smile widens, and I raise my arms to wrap them around him. I can feel Matthew's heartbeat on the rise. He's a little nervous too. He breathes in a little, then looks at me. "Is that cologne on you?" he asks.

I nod. "Yes," I say, super excited. "Thank you for noticing."

"It's really good," he says.

I give him another kiss and I get the sudden feeling that I could do this all night long, but I can't. The party is not that far from us. "So, what now?"

Matthew shushes me with his finger. "That can wait. For now, let's just enjoy the moment."

"Seriously," I say a with a little giggle. "Anyone could see us. We should really get going."

Matthew rolls his eyes. "Fine," he says, and pulls out a helmet from the seat. "Put this on and then we'll head out."

I do as I'm told and put on the helmet. It's not

that bad, though I feel like my hair will definitely get squished by it, but it's either that or have a messy hairstyle caused by the wind. Once I tighten it up, Matthew seats himself on the motorcycle. I sit right behind him and wrap my arms around his stomach. My head rests on his shoulder. Matthew looks down at me for a second. He gives me a gentle smile, and I smile back.

"You ready?" he asks.

"Yes," I say.

Matthew starts the engine, and we ride off.

15

I always dreamed of owning a motorcycle. I liked the idea of riding it at full speed with no helmet and letting the wind blow my hair back. I liked the idea, but my parents weren't exactly okay with it. They always warned me about the dangers of riding a motorcycle and how I'd most likely get killed. Mom even shared a story about how she badly skinned her knee when riding one and how they had to scrub off the torn flesh from her more than once. The thought of it brings a shiver through my spine. Yet, despite their attempts, I kept dreaming of the day I'd ride one.

Now that I'm on a bike with Matthew, I can confidently say that the whole thing goes wider than anything I could've imagined.

It all feels like something out of a romance novel.

The second we jump onto the road, Matthew tunes into a radio station, cranks up the speed and before I know it, we're riding so fast that the world around us is practically a blur. The music bursts out of the speakers and becomes one with the air, traveling in all sorts of directions and spreading its wonder to the rest of the world. The lyrics are hard to follow because of the speeding winds, but it's the sound of the beat that matters. One high adrenaline pump song that fits into the current mood.

"Click the red button on the helmet," Matthew yells to me.

"What?" I yell back.

"I said click the red button on the helmet. It'll help you hear the music better."

"And what about you?"

"Don't worry. I'll focus on the driving. You just enjoy yourself."

I search my helmet for the red button with my hand, which finds it attached to the side near my head. When I press it on, the music bursts into my ears so loud that I feel as if my eardrums are about to explode. I pat Matthew on the shoulder, and he takes it as a sign to bring down the volume. He lowers it slowly, and when it reaches a steady level, I give him a thumbs up for him to stop.

The song itself is infectious. It's irresistible garage band sounds make me want to jump around and sing off the lyrics. The lyrics don't make sense to me at all, but hey, it's still good. I tap Matthew's belly to the beat. He doesn't appear to be bothered by it. When the song comes to an end, I ask Matthew what the song title is, and make a note about it when I get an answer. "It's one of my favorites," Matthew yells to me. "It's pretty good when I feel like riding fast."

"Do you do this often?" I ask.

"Not much. I can only do this in the night when my dad is asleep."

"Didn't think you were the kind of guy that listened to this type of music or do stuff like this."

Matthew laughs. "There's a lot of things you don't know about me. Just wait 'til you see where we're going, and then you might get a clearer view of what kind of person I am."

I plant a kiss on his cheek. "I think I already have a clear idea of who you are."

Matthew smiles and before I know it, we jump onto the highway.

Thanks to the highway, we cover a lot more ground than we could on the usual roads. Within thirty minutes, we've left the open nature of our hometown behind and traded it for the urban scenery of the Baltimore area. As the city lights come into view, I lean into Matthew's ear and say, "What exactly are we going to do here?"

Matthew turns his head gently. "We're going to go dancing," he replies.

"But where, exactly?"

His lips curve into a smile. "You'll see."

Matthew takes us out of the highway and into a part of the city. Unlike the other districts like the Inner Harbor, this place feels more like if it were a small town. The buildings are not city-type tall, the road isn't so wide, and there's not that many people. The only difference is that it has that city smell, which is a mixture of burned gas and trash. There's also the view of the downtown area in the distance, with its tall buildings lit up from top to bottom.

Matthew takes a turn into an underground parking lot where we leave the bike. When we emerge, I get a much clearer view of the street. There's not much to see around here, except for a few restaurants and businesses.

"Where to next?" I ask.

"Just come with me."

Matthew takes my hand and guides me through the streets. Naturally, I'd be terrified about him holding me like this because we're out in the open, but something about being far away from home makes me feel a little bit safer. It's probably because no one here knows who I am so I can be out in the open without worrying that my parents would find out. A few people pass by us and notice our conjoined hands, but none of them say or do anything harmful. Some let us be while others smile at us. I smile back, probably out of character. For the first time since I've come out to my parents, I feel… normal.

Matthew notices me smiling and he smiles back. "It feels nice, right?" he says.

I turn to him. "What?"

"Being completely open about it. It's nice."

He doesn't mention what "it" is, but I know what he means, and he is right. It is nice, but it's weird when people turn to look at us. I honestly don't get that. We're just holding hands; no one ever looked at my parents like that when they held hands in public. But to be honest, when people look at us and give us smiles, it gives me confidence.

Still, a little part of me is still uncomfortable with the whole thing. Matthew on the other hand, seems totally okay with everything. He leads us through the streets without any sign that he's in unfamiliar territory. My face can tell people that I'm not used to this, but Matthew's, on the other hand, can definitely tell the opposite, even though he's still closeted like I am. "How are you so confident?" I finally ask him.

Matthew turns to me. "Positive thinking," he says. "It's all about not letting negativity overrun you."

I don't say anything else. Strangely, Matthew has said it all.

We keep on walking through until we come up to a street and stop in front of an alley. "Here we are," Matthew says, and I scan the surroundings. The street is quiet, with a couple of cars parked apart and some people standing or walking around. The buildings are roughly consisted of small businesses like delis and retail stores on the ground floors and apartments on the other floors. All businesses are either closed or closing and the apartments have one or two lights on. Nothing of this place suggests that there's anything we could do for fun.

I look at Matthew, who's scanning the street as if he

were trying to make sure that no one was watching us. A second after that, he pulls me with him into the darkness of the alley that we walk through until we come upon a steel door. Matthew knocks it gently and within a few seconds, the door opens slightly to show half of a bouncer's face. "Password," the bouncer says.

"True colors," Matthew says.

The bouncer shuts the door, and after a second, opens it in total. For a second, I worry that he's going to ask for some ID or something. Instead, he just says, "Come on in," and we do as we're told. We walk through a hallway until we come up to a pair of steps. From down below, I can hear the sound of loud music and people.

"Are we doing something illegal?" I ask him.

Matthew leans into me. "Don't worry," he whispers. "I've been here before and it's perfectly safe."

A part of me wonders how he's been here before, but I miss my chance to ask him when he turns around and keeps going down. I follow right behind him. The more we descended, the more the light diminished, and the more the sound of music and people got louder. As we near the bottom, Matthew turns to me and smiles. "You ready?" he says, all excitedly.

"I… don't know," I reply hesitantly.

He grabs my hand. "Don't be scared. You're about to feel more welcomed than ever before."

I have no idea what that means, but I follow him anyway.

16

When we reach the basement, my eyes widen.

The room itself has got to be at least four times the size of my home garage. In the center of the room lies a dance floor with white colored square lights that flick on and off faster than I can blink. To the side lies a bar with a series of fridges and neon lights behind it. High tables and booths surround the dancefloor, each one holding a little plastic electric candle in the center. Positioned in the back of the room is a DJ set with expensive looking equipment and super powerful speakers that are blasting music out into the room. The sounds clutter my ears. About maybe thirty or forty people—mostly teenagers—are spread out throughout the room.

An astonished "wow" escapes from my lips.

"I know," Matthew says, pulling up his camera. He lifts it to my face and takes a shot of me as my lips curve into a smile. My smile widens. He's done this before, taken pictures of me at random moments. He's got a few of us cuddling and kissing and others of just me. I've taken a few shots of him but they're not as good. Still, he says that he keeps them anyway.

"Where, exactly?" I ask.

"At home," he says. "I have them stored in a USB drive hidden in my room. Don't worry, they'll never find them."

And I trust him.

He lowers the camera and smiles at me. "Why don't you go find us a place to sit while I get us some drinks."

"Did you bring cash?" I ask.

Matthew nods and we separate. While he takes off to the bar, I go sit down in a booth where he can see me. A crowd is gathered up by the bar waiting to get served and there's only one bartender handling all of them. It looks like Matthew might be there for a while. Whatever; it's not like I'm in a hurry to drink.

I gaze at the kids on the dancefloor. Every one of them is really getting down to it, moving their bodies to the rhythm and sometimes shouting and singing off to the lyrics of the sound if they're lucky enough to be able to hear them. Some of them are gathered in groups of two or more. Some are made up of boys and others of girls, but never mixed together. My eyes fall upon this one boy with short hair who's dancing right in the center. His arms and head are lying on someone in front of him. A date most likely.

The crowd clears a bit, and I can see them a little better. My eyes widen.

His date is a boy.

"You okay?" Matthew asks. I turn to him and watch as he seats himself next to me, a drink in each hand which he sets down on the table. My eyes fall back on the two boys in the dancefloor. Matthew spots them and smiles. "Looks like fun, right?"

I look at him. "Where are we?"

Matthew takes a sip of his drink. "You could say that this is a sanctuary, of sorts. This is a place where people like us can come over and just chill and have fun without being eyed by straight people so much."

"So, you brought me to a gay bar?"

"Not exactly. It's more like a gay club for kids and adults. Here we can come in and be ourselves without fearing any judgement."

"And what about this place?" I gesture to the whole basement.

"It used to be an old speakeasy place during the Prohibition era. The owners bought it a few years ago and made a few improvements to it. Once it was sound-proof and all the paperwork was cut out, they spread the word and business started flowing in."

"But why set up shop underground?"

A small laugh escapes Matthew's lips. "Let's just say that for the right price, they'll give you something better than just waters or sodas."

I stare down at the glass in front of me. The ice cubes in it float gently in the center, and a few bubbles form from the bottom and make their way up towards the top where they pop. I grab it in my hand and sniff it a little. Nothing out of the usual. Still…

"Is there booze in this?" I ask.

Matthew leans into me. By now, he's had about four to six sips of his drink. "You tell me," he whispers before planting his lips on mine.

The kiss is nice, and it was actually a surprise that he went like that. When his tongue slips into my mouth, I begin to taste something odd out of it, and it's not his saliva. It tasted like something that made me think of my grandfather and how he always ordered his waters with a splash of vodka. Is that what it is? Did Matthew just have a sip before kissing me? I ask him that when we separate. "Yeah," he says honestly.

"Does mine have booze as well?" I ask.

Matthew nods. "You don't have to drink it if you don't want to. Though I would suggest you do."

"Why?"

"Because you'll loosen up a bit. Then you can have a bit of fun."

I look at the drink in hand. "I don't know…"

"Come on," he whines. "Just try it."

I roll my eyes and raise the glass to my mouth. When the liquid touches my lips, I open up to let the tiniest sip of it slip inside. The moment it's in my mouth is the moment that my taste buds react. It was as if I was tasting some acid-like liquid. I feel like spitting it back on the glass, but instead, I swallow it down. After that, I look at Matthew. "How much booze are in these?" I ask.

"Not much," he says. "There's only a splash of it so we can get a little loose, but don't drink too much. It'll only ruin the night."

"So, what now?"

Matthew grabs his glass. "For now, we keep drinking."

We clank our glasses and keep drinking. Within a few minutes, we finish them and by then, I'm feeling the alcohol's effect already. My head feels a bit lighter, and my body starts feeling numb. I start losing my control on what I say, and I feel a little happier than usual. I'm actually liking this feeling. My parents never let me have even one sip of booze and if they ever found out about this, they would've no doubt chew me off hard for it. But who cares?

I think I need to sober up now.

"Can we get some water or something?" I ask Matthew.

Matthew gives me a semi-drunken smile. "Later," he says playfully. "Let's go dance."

Matthew drags me onto the dancefloor without any resistance from me. There, he lets himself loose. He raises his arms to the air and moves his body in ways that I never imagined. I follow his lead, but my focus is mainly tied to him. This is the first time I see him dance, and I have to admit, he's really good. Also, something about his movements are just so... sexy. I blush.

Matthew stops for a moment and watches me dance. I have my arms raised and moving around. My body twists and turns from side to side. He watches me with awe and lifts his camera up. Before I know it, he's taking shots of me. My smile widens.

Eventually, he lowers his camera and smiles. Then, he takes me by the hand and drags me closer to his body. Our chests crash into each other as we wrap our arms around one another. A leg of his is positioned in between mine. His face is so close to mine that I can feel his breath touch my face. A shiver runs through me. Our eyes are on each other, drawn together by the cosmic force of admiration.

"Can I have this dance?" Matthew asks.

I smile at him. "You bet your butt you can."

We dance, so close that our movements are not that much. Matthew shakes us from side to side, occasionally rotating his hip and mine in the process. His hands run through my back, and I do the same. At a certain point, he brings his hand down to my butt and squeezes it. I jump a little bit and he laughs. Then, I lean forward and kiss his neck. He pulls me in deeper, pressing me into his neck and getting me to kiss him harder.

The whole thing feels sexual. My chest is aching

for him, and with every kiss, touch and move, the fire intensifies, and I don't want it to stop. I want more. I want to kiss him harder and go down on him all over again, just like when we were in his room. I wonder if we can sneak into some bathroom or closet. No, too risky. *Keep it in your pants*, I tell myself.

The current song ends and a new one begins playing, a slow song. Matthew releases me a little bit and after our legs untangle, we wrap our arms around one another and start to dance. We move our hips from side to side, slowly. Our eyes are on each other again. This time, we don't lose focus.

Even though we moved passed the whole hormonal, sexually fueled dance or whatever, my chest is still burning. Outside, it all seems normal. But within me, there's an internal struggle between me and the impulse to kiss him. I try to concentrate on other things, but my thoughts keep going back to him, with his bright eyes, his perfect smile and his beautiful facial features that make me smile even if he was angry with me. Not that he's ever gotten angry with me, but still…

Another slow song commences. This one I recognize: a duet between Marvin Gaye and Tammi Terrell. It's complex yet irresistible opening begins to play, then

Gaye's voice—followed by Terrell's—bursts out singing. Matthew and I dance to it, never parting and so close to each other that I can feel his body heat. I look into his eyes. They sparkle, even more so in the darkness. I blush.

Maybe it's the alcohol getting to me, but I feel like this is the right time to tell him. Our hands are on each other, we're close together and we're acting silly and having fun. What better moment than—

My stomach churns. "Where's the bathroom?" I ask Matthew.

Matthew points a finger and I immediately run in the same direction.

17

I'm lucky that I was able to reach a toilet in time. Once I'm done puking my brains out, I come out of it feeling way worse than before, obviously because my stomach's empty.

My first instinct is to get something in me. Maybe I should try to get to the bar and order something to eat, and maybe two or three glasses of water. A part of me thinks that I don't have the strength to even walk out of the bathroom. Hell, I barely have the energy to keep standing. Maybe I should just lie down on the floor here. Nope, too sticky and it smells bad. I'd rather throw up again.

I settle for drinking water out of the bathroom sink. I drag my wasted ass over to the counter and immediately turn the sink handle. Just as the water starts to pour out, I bend my head down and start chugging as much as I can with my mouth and tongue. I lift a hand up and direct more water over to my mouth. I splash some on my face as well. Thankfully, it helps clear my eyes. *God, this feels so good*, I tell myself.

After two or three minutes, my mind has sharpened, my headache has slightly gone away, and I feel a little less dehydrated. I stand up straight and look at myself in the mirror. I'm still wasted; I see it in my eyes. They don't exactly show that I'm on my A-game. I splash some cold water on my face and then proceed to dry myself up with my shirt.

It's only as I finish up drying up my face that I hear the door open.

"Taylor," an all too familiar voice says from behind.

My eyes widen. I turn around my jaw drops.

Standing in front of me is a boy who's definitely my age. He's wearing a pair of tattered black trousers, a faded dark gray t-shirt, and a sleeveless leather jacket. His hands are covered by a pair of fingerless gloves, revealing his dirty fingernails. His brown hair is covered by a black torn beanie. If anything, he looks somewhat like Matthew, if Matthew had taken a bad boy look to a whole new level.

But neither of those details shock me as much as his face, a face I haven't seen in a long time, six months to be precise.

"Kyle," I say unbelievably.

Kyle doesn't say anything. Instead, he steps forward to me and sweeps me into a hug. A series of emotions goes through me—shock, disbelief, joy—and all of it happens as he has me take in the realization that I'm not imagining any of this. *This is real,* my mind tells me. *Kyle is here, in front of me, hugging me, really here.*

One question burns in my head though. "How?"

"I escaped," Kyle says as he sets me loose.

"*Escaped?*" It sounds unbelievable, but he's here. He's out in the world, in front of me, actually free.

"I know. It sounds crazy, but it's true."

"But your parents…" I stop myself. Of course, they'd obviously lie about it. I have no doubt that if I got out as well, my dad would've kept it secret for appearances and who knows what. "What are you doing here?" I ask.

"What are *you* doing here?" he asks me back before his eyes widen. "Wait, are you—"

"Yeah," I say. I knew what he was going to ask me from the start. Me being here is already a big giveaway.

Kyle snaps out of his shock. "Sorry. It's just… wow. I didn't expect that from you. No offense."

"None taken."

Kyle scratches the back of his head. "I wish I'd known that long ago. Still, what are you doing here?"

"I could ask you the same thing."

Kyle rolls his eyes. "Alright. Answer me first and then I'll go."

I tell Kyle everything—how I was questioning for a while, how I came out to my parents, how they reacted, and how I met Matthew. When I started talking about Matthew, Kyle's interest had peaked. He listened to every word, put all the pieces together, and read between the lines. When I finished, he said, "I didn't expect you to have that sort of luck." He sighs. "Wish I'd been as careful as you. Maybe I wouldn't be here."

"Which brings me to now," I say. "Why are you here?"

Kyle sighs. "I'm here because I'm safe," he says, which barely makes any sense to me whatsoever. I raise an eyebrow as he says, "Why don't we sit down, and I can explain things a little better."

Kyle guides me towards a bench pressed to the bathroom wall. Why they have a bench here, I will never know. When I sit down and look at him, I get a better view of his face, which has changed a little bit. His facial features had switched up a bit, already showing the signs of a young man. Apart from that, I think the main thing that's changed are his eyes. They still have the same dark brown tone that looks like dirt, but behind them was a series of emotions that might as well describe the past six months to me. Pain, fear, a little bit of sadness; they were all written through them, but he's not shedding any tears, trembling, biting his nails or even looking in any sort of way like he's in pain.

He looks… totally calm.

"So, you already know how my parents found out about my sexuality and how they send me off," he begins. "They took me to this clinic roughly three hours away from town against my will. I didn't realize where we were heading until it was too late. My first thought was to make a break for it the first chance I got, but we never stopped once. Even when we were stuck in traffic my dad kept the locks on. I tried phoning someone, but they took that from me the second they had the chance. I had no way to get out, and it was then that I started to panic.

"Anyway, by the time we got there, a bunch of doctors and nurses were waiting for me. I looked at my parents and asked them why they were doing this, and they said that it was for my own good and whatnot. When they handed me to the doctors, I tried to fight them off but one of them injected me with something and before I knew it, I passed out. I woke up a while later in a cell with no windows. By then, I knew that it was too late for me to escape."

Kyle pauses and looks down. It's not easy for him, opening up about something so harsh that it can hardly be imagined unless you live through it. I place a hand on his shoulder. He looks up at me. He gives me a slight nod and continues.

"After that, it was the usual stuff you'd go through in places like that. There were tons of group therapy sessions, one on one therapy sessions, pills I was forced to swallow, and a daily dose of electroshock treatment. That last part was the worst. You have no idea what it's like to get a dozen jolts of electricity jammed into your brain until they actually do it, and let me tell you, it really, *really* hurts."

His body shivers but he pressures on. "My parents occasionally came to visit, twice a month at least. I begged them to let me come home, but they wouldn't see the light. They kept saying how it was all for my own good and even spoke about how it's worked on other people and all sorts of crap. I tried to tell them that I didn't want to change and that this was hurting me, but they didn't care. Even if I did have signs of abuse on me or proof of what they said and did to me, they'd still leave me in there."

It's at this point that I notice how he's holding back some tears. I stroke a hand gently over his back before pulling him into a hug. With that, he cracks. Tears stream down his cheeks and gently crash onto my forearm. I keep stroking his back, which only happens to bring more tears out, but at least gets him to let it all out. I tighten my hold on him and rest my head on his shoulder. Kyle does the same and we stay like that for a while.

Once it's all out, Kyle lets go of me. He wipes the tears from his face and says, "After a while, I gave up trying to convince them to see the light and I also gave up on finding a way out. There was too much security. A chain link fence with barbed wire on the top surrounded the compound and there were dozens of guards all over the place. No one who was admitted was allowed to leave without receiving a confirmation from their parents. The place might as well be a prison, which now that I think about it, is actually what it was. I was trapped there, and it seemed impossible to break out, or so I thought."

I lean in a little closer. "What happened?" I ask.

Kyle smiles. "While I was there, I met this guy Dave in one of the group therapy sessions. He was admitted about five weeks before I was, and he'd been planning his escape since day one. We bonded in such a short time, and once he knew that I wasn't fully committed to the clinic's program like some of the others, he offered to take me with him when he escaped. I said yes, obviously, and that's when he filled me in on his plan. Funny fact: the clinic does this field trip to this little place where nearby communities hold some church retreats. That was our ticket out.

"The retreat was simple: something to get us into seeing the truth about how God can save us and all that. The place is pretty isolated and surrounded by woods in all directions. The clinic sends guards along with the kids, but not that many. That last part was the main thing. Without that many guards, we only had to run as far from them as possible in order for them to lose us. The trip only happens twice a year, and thankfully, the next one was scheduled for a week from then. All I had to do was wait.

"When the day came, Dave made sure to keep track of the route we took to get there to see if we could find any nearby town to make our next moves. When we got there, he told me to wait for him to tell him when the time was right and to just suck up whatever they said. And so, I did. I listened to every annoying chat, lecture and group therapy session that came and waited for him to say something. During a lecture, he told me that he was going to the bathroom. 'Wait five minutes and then go there too,' he told me. I did as he said, and after five minutes I asked and went.

"On the way over there, I was escorted by a guard and then handed to another guard who said I had to wait for Dave to come out. That's where the interesting part came. Dave didn't come out at all, not voluntarily or when the guard told him that time was up. When he went in to find out what was taking him so long, Dave… attacked him. I'm not gonna to go into full details but let's just say that he managed to beat the shit out of him with a plunger. I know, crazy, but it took the guard down. He grabbed whatever he had in his pocket, which in this case was a bit of cash and his weapon—a gun with rubber bullets—and then he pulled the fire alarm.

"Everyone was quickly evacuated, and no one bothered to look for us. Dave guided me through the building until we came across an emergency exit through the back. We went through it, and before I knew it, we were running for our lives through the woods. I think they went searching for us. I thought I felt that someone was chasing us. Thankfully, they didn't catch up to us.

"Dave and I came out of the woods a while later, and we—or I should say he—carjacked someone and we took off to the city. From there, we ditched the car and came here. There were people here who knew Dave and offered to help him. Since then, we've just been moving around the city, never looking back and always keeping our heads down. So, that's it. End of story."

I'm… at a loss for words. For him to go through all that, and not fall apart in all the chances that he could've is just… Wow. Crazy. A shiver runs through my spine. I look at Kyle and see it all over again; all the pain that he had gone through and had overcome. He seems reborn, as if the old him had been dead for quite some time and replaced with this new version.

A stronger version.

"How have you been?" I ask him, which is all I can think of saying to him now.

Kyle raises an eyebrow. "How do you think I'm doing?" he replies a little aggressive.

I back away a little. "Whoa. Sorry."

"Sorry," he says calmly. "I haven't been asked that in so long, so it feels weird. And I'm sorry for the attitude. Kinda got that from having to look after myself." He turns to me. "And to answer your question, I'm doing okay. I mean I may be living in a shelter, but I'm still good."

"Are you alone?"

He shakes his head. "Dave is with me. We've had each other's back since we got out, and there's a few other people in a shelter that have been helping us." He studies my face. "You don't need to worry about me. I'm doing alright. Struggling a bit, but still alright."

"Still, do you need any help? I could see if I can—"

"No," he breaks in. "It's okay. I'll be fine. Just look after yourself and don't worry much about me. Besides, Dave and I are actually leaving."

"Leaving? Where?"

"They're moving us to another shelter up north. They say that it's for our protection and to be honest,

I think the further I get from my parents and those bastards from the clinic, the better." He looks down at his watch. "I gotta go. It was really nice seeing you. I hope things go better for you." He gets up and heads for the door.

"Wait," I tell him. Kyle turns around. "Will I ever see you again?"

Kyle's expression changes. "Maybe. I'm not sure."

I honestly believe the same thing. "Well, is there any advice you'd give me on what to do?"

Kyle smiles. "Just love yourself and keep fighting for what you want. That's all I can think of."

I know I barely knew Kyle, but I raise my arms and pull him into a hug.

18

I walk out of the bathroom to find Matthew waiting for me in front of the door. "There you are," he says. "I was worried about you."

I smile and kiss him on the cheek. "No need to worry anymore," I whisper into his ear. "I'm right here."

Matthew laughs. "That may be true, but you're definitely still wasted. Come on."

Matthew drags me by the hand towards the bar where he orders me a glass of water. Three minutes later, the glass is empty, and he orders me another one, which I empty again. After the third glass of water, I start to feel a little better, but still pretty drunk. "Your stomach's most likely empty," Matthew says to me. "I know a good pizza place if you're up for it."

I nod and we leave the club. Half an hour later,

we're sitting in a table chowing down on these slices that are about twice the size of the ones the pizzeria back home offers. I take one in my hand and carefully guide it to my mouth. With the first bite, I'm like, *Oh my God! That's amazing*, which it really is. Maybe it's the cheese or the pepperoni, but I find myself stuffing the whole thing in my mouth, even when there isn't any more room. It's kind of a problem with me. If something is really good, I basically can't help myself but to have it all in me.

Matthew watches and laughs. "What?" I say with my mouth half full.

"Nothing," he says. "You just have some grease on your face." He gestures a finger to the corners of his mouth.

I wipe my mouth with a napkin. "Sorry," I say.

Matthew looks at me. "Is this how you usually eat pizza?"

I raise my shoulders. "Only when it's really good."

Matthew laughs. "Well, I will admit, watching you chow down on half the pizza in less than ten minutes has been one hell of a show. No offense."

I smile. "None taken." I gesture to the remaining four slices. "You gonna eat that?"

Matthew shakes his head. "No. Help yourself if you want to."

"Thanks, but I'm already full. Should we—" I stop myself. I was gonna ask if we should take it, but I already know the answer.

"We can't," Matthew says. "My parents or yours will notice that it's not from town and they'll ask questions."

I sigh. "Well, at least it was a good pizza. Doubt it'll taste the same once we defrost it."

"True." A minute of silence. "By the way, I've been meaning to ask you something."

I look at him. "What is it?"

"Back in the bathroom. What exactly took you so long? I've had my own experiences with throwing up after getting wasted, but it certainly didn't take me that long."

I bite my lip and immediately think back to Kyle. His face comes back to me through my thoughts. He had changed since the last time I saw him, and even the way he acted around me was different. The last word he said to me was "maybe" and he left without even saying goodbye. We weren't that close when we were younger, but we still knew and talked to each other. But six months apart had changed him, and now that I think of it, I've changed as well.

Knowing how Matthew's family plays an important role in town and all the loose lips that are in town, they must have already heard about Kyle. In any case, I guess I should tell him.

And so, I do. I tell him about Kyle, explaining what he told me and shared everything that went through my head as it happened. Matthew paid close attention and when I finished, he took a deep breath and said, "Do you think he needs our help?"

I shake my head. "He said that I didn't need to worry about him and it seemed as if he wasn't gonna tell me what he needs even if I pressured him into it. I just hope he doesn't get caught."

"And are they still looking for him?"

"He didn't say, but he did escape, so his parents must know, which means that they probably are. They're moving him up north along with his friend Dave, and he said that I might see him again, but I'm not so sure." My mind goes back to thinking about what he said that they did at the clinic, and I wonder if my dad knows about that. He most likely doesn't. The clinic wouldn't put that in their brochure. But if he does know, would he still send me away? Is he really capable of that?

Matthew takes notice of my worried face. "That'll never happen to us," he says.

I raise an eyebrow. "How do you know?"

Matthew smiles. "Because I have faith," he says, which honestly, felt like the only reason I needed.

The night ends at my front door. We pay for the pizza, get back to the parking lot and ride back to town. We get there around 10:30pm, and fifteen minutes later, we stop in front of my house. It was Matthew's choice to drop me off at home. He said he didn't want me walking alone at night, which honestly was very thoughtful of him. I had my doubts about it because my dad might be home, but when we got there, his car wasn't there, which brought me a sense of relief. Matthew also made sure to keep the noise down, so no one notices us coming in, and thankfully, no one peeked out the windows to see what was going on.

Matthew turns the engine off as soon as we come to a stop. We disembark from the bike, and he proceeds to park it. "So," he tells me. "What do you think? Best night ever or what?"

I take my helmet off and smile. "This was definitely a night I'll never forget."

Matthew smiles. "I'm gonna take that as a sign that you had fun."

A minute of silence. Then I say, "I've been meaning to ask you something. How did you know of that club?"

Matthew's expression changes. "Well, I grew up in the city a while back. My dad was there doing some work at a church before we came here. It was around that time that I was coming to realize about my attraction to boys. There was this guy at school, John, who apparently noticed it and to this day I don't know how. He helped me out a bit and one night he took me there, which as where I was able to feel more comfortable about the whole thing and actually get a break from my dad's control. I felt… free."

I take a step forward towards him. "I can see that already. It was really fun."

"I know." He avoids my eyesight for a second. "I should probably tell you that up until that night, I had never kissed a boy."

"You had you first kiss down there?"

"Don't get too excited. I was young, foolish, blinded by love, and I…" Matthew sighs. "I wasted it."

Matthew lowers his head and avoids looking at me.

"What happened?" I ask him.

He looks up and begins. "As you already know, John took me down there one night. When we went there, we had a few drinks and... umm... to put it simply, I kissed him. I was super drunk, and I just did it because he was like my first love and honestly, I felt like he was the one. He umm... he didn't love me back. By the time he said that it was too late. I kissed him, told him I loved him, poured my heart out to him and despite that, he didn't feel the same way."

Matthew holds back a sob. "Anyway, I got over it, but it hurt for quite a bit. It really hurts when someone doesn't love you back, especially when that someone is your first love." He sighs. "After that, I just became a bit reclusive about my feelings. I didn't want to get hurt again and all, but then you came and... well, I opened my heart up to you. I know what it sounds like, but I couldn't help myself, because... I love you."

My insides tingle. Butterflies flap in my stomach. He said he loves me, more times than I can count, and I haven't said it back once. I've told him other stuff, simple compliments, and whatnot, but 'I love you' hasn't yet come out of my mouth. I think I should say it now, or I might never get another chance.

"Look," Matthew says, "I'm sorry for oversharing or something. I just—"

"No. It's okay. I just… I didn't expect that." A few seconds of silence. "I want you to know something.

Matthew raises his head to me. "Shoot."

I take a deep breath. "I want you to know that I'll never make you feel like that. And I want you to know that you don't have to worry about being let down." I grab his hand and squeeze it gently. "I'm here now, and I love you."

And there it is. I told him that I love him, and I meant it. All I can say is that it was worth it. All the hiding, secrecy, and good times that made me say it mean something to me.

I turn to Matthew, who's still looking at me. His eyes sparkle with the moonlight, but something else shone through them. It looked new and fresh, as if it were born right this second. Maybe it was there all along, and it had just been waiting to come out at the right time. He looks at me with this new feeling going through him and smiles. "I love you too," he says, then proceeds to kiss me.

All my life, I've dreamt of having something close to a fairy tale. Now that I have it, everything else in life feels like it'll fall into place. Nothing can stop it.

Around an hour before midnight, my mom gets home from wherever she was. I'm in my room getting ready for bed when I hear the front door open. She calls me from downstairs. "Taylor," she says. "Could you come down here?"

I go downstairs to find my mom sitting in the couch. Her legs are close together and her hands rest on her lap. Her posture is straight, as if she were trying to be serious. None of that is like her. She only does that on one occasion and it's never a good sign.

"Is something wrong?" I ask her.

My mom doesn't answer. "Can you please sit?" She gestures to the empty spot next to her.

I sit beside her without hesitating and stare at her. The look on her face tells me that something happened. Was it about dad? It had to be. He isn't here yet and that's so unlike him. Her lip twitches and I notice how she pricks on a nail.

"What's going on?"

My mom lowers my head and takes my hand. "I want you to know that none of what's going to happen is your fault," she says. "What's happening is between me and your father and it's all in your best interest."

My heartbeat kicks up. "Okay, you're scaring me. What are you talking about?"

My mom caresses my hand, closes her eyes, takes a deep breath, and speaks.

"I'm divorcing your father."

19

For a brief moment, I freeze. My eyes widen, my body tenses up, and my spine shivers. "What?" escapes my lips. My mind is spinning like crazy. A divorce? Really? I didn't see that coming.

Mom clears up my confusion. Apparently, she and dad had a fight regarding me and what to do about my sexuality and it got pretty heated. "He wanted me to jump into the idea that we should get you to see a doctor or something," she says and pauses for a minute. "I… I tried to get him to see reason, honey. I really, really tried, but he just doesn't want to. He's always been stubborn but now it's like it's gone through the roof. So, I'm done with him."

"But…" My voice falters. I can't actually think of any reason for why she shouldn't. Besides, why would

I defend him? He deserves it. He's been planning to send me away since all this came to light. If anything, I would do the same thing if I were her. I'd up stakes and leave, never to return.

But he's still my father. He loves me—in a way—and this is my family. I'm not going to let it be broken.

"Are you sure you can't give him more time?" I ask her.

My mom lowers her head. "I have given him time. Time after time I've told him to stop talking crazy, to reflect on it, to maybe go see a shrink, but he just won't do any of those things. Nothing I do is going to make him change. I'm through with him."

"But do you still love him?"

She looks at me uncomfortably. "I do, but I need to protect you as well and if he's going to send you away for something so silly, then he'll have to take you away from me."

Despite the current situation, I find myself smiling. She's willing to sacrifice her relationship with my father for my safety. Never again will I doubt if she really loves me. I take her hand and caress it. "Thank you," I say. "But you gotta know that love's not a light switch. Getting dad to accept me is gonna take some time and if you get divorced, you might as well be giving up on him."

My mother looks at me shockingly. She takes in what I said and then raises me a weak smile. "When did you start being so hopeful about all this?"

Because I've been dating Matthew in secrecy and it has been a major experience, I wanted to say. But instead, I say, "I just don't want to see this family break apart," and leave it there.

Mom stayed downstairs for a bit and, while she took a moment to think about it, I go into their room and searched dad's file compartment for the papers. In the middle of the stack in the file under my name is where I find them: papers to a conversion clinic here in the state. I google the place and take in all the details. Founded in 1926, specializes in psychological disorders and contains one simple yet fully equipped conversion therapy program. No records of how many people were actually "cured" were shown. I gulp.

I find it hard to fall asleep after that. Thoughts about the whole thing were running through my brain that I couldn't find a way to ignore. Mom says that she has the situation under control, but now it seems like her control of things is slipping away. At least the papers say that both parents must sign the paperwork to send me away, so there's good news in that. But if dad goes to change it to only need his authorization, then I'm screwed. I wonder if I should just run away. Nope, can't do it.

I can't leave my home and I can't leave Matthew.

I think of any possibility or excuse that would make me stay hopeful, but it all comes to an end when I fall asleep. Thankfully, I don't get any bad dreams, or any dreams for that matter, and when I'm awoken for the Sunday sermon, I crawl out of bed and put on my Sunday best. I come out of my room with jeans and a polo shirt and proceed downstairs to eat breakfast. Mom is already there, cooking up a storm of eggs and bacon. She gives me some and I sit down to eat.

Halfway through my breakfast, dad comes into the room dressed in a suit and tie. He grabs a plate and fills it with a share of food and sits in front of me. An exchange of glances soon follow: first him to mom, then him to me. When he looks at me, my spine shivers. His anger and disappointment haven't gone away one bit. If anything, they've stayed where they've been since day one. He doesn't breathe a word until he says that we have to go. Mom proceeds to put the plates in the dishwasher and head out the door.

Thankfully, the ride goes quickly and with no heated arguments. A few words were passed on between my parents, but there was no concrete conversation. Mom avoids his eyesight, and she occasionally turns to look at her as if trying to discover what he did wrong. I wonder if he already knows about mom's plans to divorce him. He probably doesn't. She hasn't told him yet, but she will, if he doesn't change his mind about conversion therapy. *Their marriage is doomed,* my mind tells me.

No, it's not, I say back, but to be honest, mom makes a point. She's tried and tried and tried to get him to see reason. Nothing has worked so I can tell why she's tired. Maybe it's for the best that they get divorced. I'd be safe, obviously, which is the main reason that she's doing this. Still, my safety would cause her to leave the man she loves. Once that happens, there's no turning back.

I need a break from thinking about this. I pull out my phone and text Matthew.

> **Me:** Need to see u after church. You free after?
> **Matthew:** Sure. The house will be empty so

we can have some privacy.
Me: Thank u. <<smiling emoji>>

Matthew and I meet out in front of the church grounds after telling my mom that I'll be hanging out with him. His mom drops us off back at his place and then heads out to run some errands. Matthew's father is going to come in late because of a meeting, but she said that she'll be back in like three hours. "You two behave," she tells us, and then takes off. Matthew and I have the house to ourselves.

We head up to his room where we kick off our shoes and make ourselves comfortable. Matthew opts for the bed while I take his desk chair. My eyes fall on him as he lays in his bed all comfortable and happy. My lips curve into a smile. It's still hard to believe that it's only been a while since we kissed, and not too long after that, he went down on me.

The moment comes back to me in a flash. The kissing, the touching, the passion; all of it makes my skin feel warm. I want it again, and I want—

Nope. Not now. I didn't come here for that. I came here because I need a break from yesterday's drama. Most kids who have divorced parents act out or shut down, but I'd rather get some comfort from someone

I love.

Matthew looks up at me. "So, what's up?" he asks.

I don't hold back. "My mom's divorcing my father," I say.

Matthew's eyes widen and after sitting up straight, he asks, "What happened?"

I explain to him what my mom told me, and I tell him about the papers I found. I tell him about how I said that she should give him more time, and how I think that she won't do it. When I finish, I find myself tearing up. Matthew gets up and gives me a hug. "It's okay," he says, caressing my back. "I'm here. Everything's going to be okay."

I sniff. "How would you know," I say bitterly. "Your parents aren't fighting over you." Immediately, I regret saying that. "I'm sorry. I just… I can't deal with this anymore." I wipe the tears from my face.

Matthew rubs a hand on my cheek. "I know," he says. "I know."

I take a deep breath. "I mean I just wish that my dad would love me. Is asking to be loved and appreciated for who I am too much?"

Matthew strokes my back. "I think you deserve more than that."

I look into Matthew's eyes. Something about them just makes me feel like they have the answers to everything. Maybe it's magic, maybe it's love. Maybe it's both at the same time. Whatever it is, I'm drawn to it.

I see the same spark that I saw when we were in here the first time. It's the same spark that made me think he was into me and the same one I saw following all that has happened after that moment between us. A smile rests on Matthew's face. My skin trembles. He says that I deserve more than love and appreciation, but I think that he's all I need.

I lean forward and press my lips to his. The kiss is soft, and sweet, and very, *very* fiery. I raise my arms and wrap them around him. My hands search for his spine. I touch it with my fingertips. Matthew shivers a little before he goes back to kissing me. He raises a hand up to my head and starts playing around with my hair, retreating his fingers like if he were massaging my scalp.

It's nice, all of it, and it's not enough. I want more than this. I want him in a different way. More… intimately.

Matthew picks up the signals because he lunges towards the bed where we come crashing down together. Our lips separated for a bit before I leaned in and kissed him again. This time, it's a lot stronger, as if I were hungry for it. Matthew kisses me, and not long after that, his tongue slips into my mouth. I press it to mine and savor it. I press his head closer to me and when his hair is in my face, I breathe in the scent. God, it's amazing.

Matthew lifts my shirt up and I lift up his. We toss them aside as our chest collide with each other. The heat from his skin is intoxicating. Matthew kisses me harder on my lips, my cheeks, and my neck. Around my neck, he gives a couple of slight kisses before biting in a little bit, not too hard so that it doesn't leave a mark. I grab his head and bring it closer to my neck. It's good, all of it.

I can feel his skin trembling as I touch it. He's… shy. I feel relieved by knowing that. I'm as scared as he is. Seeing each other like this, in a whole new way, is exactly what it should be: scary. But it's also meant to be something exciting and special. Something that gives birth to a whole new connection.

I want this, and it seems that he also does. I kiss him harder.

Matthew finds the zipper of my pants. I find his. We lower them and unbutton our pants and pull them off each other. We toss them aside and tangle up our legs. With our chests on one another, I can feel his heartbeat. It's through the roof. Matthew runs a hand over my chest. When he reaches the center, he feels my heartbeat.

"Are you nervous?" he asks.

I nod.

"Me too," he says.

I take his hand into mine. "We don't have to do this if you don't want to."

"I want to," he says. "Do you?"

I nod, and he kisses me again.

The next two hours are all hazy, but I can still remember all the kissing, touching, and moving. My favorite part of it all was when we lay down tired and we cuddled up together. Matthew's head lay on the pillow while mine rested on his chest. His heart's still beating like crazy, and his skin is covered in a mixture of heat and sweat. I love it.

I want to stay here longer. I want to keep cuddling with him, feel him, breathing him in, but I can't. My parents must now be wondering where I am and what I'm doing, and I've already received a text from mom asking such questions. I tell Matthew about this, who looks down at me and says, "It's okay. I understand." I can see the sadness in his eyes. He wants me to stay, but he knows that I can't.

We put our clothes on, and from there, we take off. Matthew's mom arrived early, and Matthew asked to borrow the car to take me home. She hands him the key with no questions. Thankfully, she doesn't notice anything that would hint out what happened between us. We walk out the door before she finds any clues.

We ride in silence and as Matthew focuses on the road ahead, I try to distract myself with the passing scenery. My mind doesn't cooperate. Everything we did is still burnt in it, replaying itself over and over again as if it were some sort of loophole. At least it's a good one. Thinking of his skin touching mine makes me feel good and having him wrapped around me makes me never want the moment to end. But that's all over now. We can't stay in that moment forever, but we made it count.

My house comes into view in just about fifteen minutes. When we stop in front of it, Matthew turns the engine off and gets out with me. We walk as far as my mailbox before he stops me. "Was it too much?" he asks. The same question as the last time.

I turn to him. "No," he says.

"Okay," he says. "I'm just making sure. I didn't want to keep on going thinking that I messed you up or something."

"Why would I be messed up or something?"

"Because we just had sex right after you told me what was happening with your family." His face looks a little panicked.

I take one of his hands into mine. "It's okay. I'm okay. I made the first move; I chose to keep going and I don't regret it. Not now, not ever."

My words speak to Matthew, who stops looking so worried and begins to smile. He leans in and plants a kiss on my cheek. I smile at him and press my lips to his, just for a second, before I move away. It's only as I move away that I see a change in him. His eyes have widened, he's biting his lip and he looks as if he just got caught. It's only then that I realize that he isn't looking at me. He's looking *behind* me.

"*Taylor*," my dad's voice calls from behind. "Inside, now."

Shit.

20

Naturally, my first instinct is to run. I'd jump into the car with Matthew and drive out of this town, never to return. Where we'll go, I'm not sure but it ought to be better than staying here.

But none of that happens. Instead, I go into the house with no protests or explanations. There's nothing I could say or do that would change what he saw. He saw us. He saw us kissing! It's a miracle that he doesn't do anything to me as I pass him by, or after he closes the door behind me.

We head into the living room where my dad finally speaks. "How long?" he asks coldly.

I'm paralyzed with fear. I feel like there's something climbing up my throat. Is it bile or my heart? I feel hot and... Am I sweating? Why am I sweating? *'Cause your secret's out, that's why*, my mind tells me.

"*How long?*" dad repeats. I can sense that he's holding back a lot of anger. "How long has this been going on?"

By "this", he means my relationship with Matthew. I swallow some bile. "Umm…"

"Umm…"

No use in denying it. "Three weeks."

My dad's eyes widen. "You've been going at this for almost a *whole month*?" His voice is elevated.

I nod fearfully.

My dad scowls. "Go to your room."

"Dad—"

"I said go to your room," he repeats.

"Dad, please—"

"I said *go to your room*."

I go to my room. There's no use in reasoning with him. He's angry, deeply angry, and trying to reason with him will only make things worse. It's better if I let him cool down now. What the hell am I thinking? He's not going to cool down. He's going to explode.

It's a miracle that he didn't yell at me, slap me, or beat me up. It's a miracle he hasn't said anything about me not seeing Matthew again or staying away from him. It's a bigger miracle that he hasn't said anything about sending me off to the conversion clinic.

Perhaps he still will.

My room is where I stay for the rest of the day. Not once do I leave except for when I went downstairs to get a sandwich and my dad ordered me to go back upstairs. He came upstairs shortly after that. He took my phone, my computer, and anything else that had a screen, leaving me with no way of getting in contact with Matthew. With only six hours before nightfall, I pass the majority of the time taking a nap.

About maybe an hour later, I wake up to the sounds of yelling. I hear the voices of my parents coming from downstairs, arguing so loud that I can hear it through a closed-door. It's muffled, but it's clear enough that I know they're talking about me. By now, my mom must know about me and Matthew, and based on how they keep arguing, I'm guessing that mom's trying to bring dad down a notch.

They go at it for a while, and then, I hear a door slam and a car engine ignite. When I look out the window, I see dad driving out of view in his car. I exhale in relief. At least I don't have to deal with him now. But where's he going? Is he going to tell Matthew's parents about us? Maybe he already did, and Matthew's now dealing with the impact of the situation.

I think of Matthew and start wondering what his parents might be telling him. I can't imagine him being discovered by my dad and then arriving at his house to find his parents disappointed in him. Maybe they started to pray, or maybe they tried to tell him that he might just be confused. Maybe they did the same thing as my dad, and they locked him up in his room. God, I wish I had my phone right now.

About a minute after dad left, mom comes up to my room. She stands in the doorway, her hands behind her, and looks at me oddly. "Hi," she says.

"Hi," I say cautiously.

She takes a few steps in. "I uh… I just wanted to give this back to you." She pulls my phone out of her pocket. I take it and say thank you. "So, uh… You and Matthew."

I lower my head.

"I'm sorry," she says. "I just wasn't expecting this anytime soon." She walks towards me and places a hand on my shoulder. I shiver. "I still love you. I'm your mother. I've always been your mother and I will never stop loving you."

I look at her and smile. She smiles back at me, and I immediately hug her. For a while, I hold on to her, and she caresses me gently as I sob a little. We separate as soon as I felt a little better. "You uh… You don't have a problem with it?" I ask.

She runs a hand through my cheek. "Not as big as your father. I'm still trying to get used to this new side of you, and I guess I didn't think that you'd be getting a boyfriend so soon after you came out."

I scratch my head. "Yeah, I didn't expect us to get together so soon, but here we are."

My mom smiles. "So, do you love him?"

I nod. "With all my heart."

"Then I'm okay with that. I don't care what your father thinks. If you're happy, I'm happy."

I smile at her. "Thank you." A few second of silence. "Say, where did dad go?"

My mom's expression changes. "He went off to the motel just outside of town. I uh… I kicked him out of the house."

My eyes widen.

"Don't look at me like that," she said. "He was planning on sending you off to the clinic and I sure as hell wasn't going to let that happen. I told him that he'll never lay a finger on you and that I'll fight him in court for your custody."

"So, you're actually going to divorce him?"

She nods gently. "Yes, I am, and it doesn't matter to me anymore. He's not the man I thought he was. What matters is you. I'm not gonna let him hurt you."

I'm both happy and sad if that's even possible. My eyes start watering. I wasn't looking forward to the divorce, but at least it means that I'll be safe from my dad, as long as he doesn't get custody. He'll never get it. I have to believe that. But what if? What if he actually gets custody?

What then?

"You think dad might win?" I ask her.

"I'm not sure, but for now, we're going to sort out our living situations before that happens." A minute of silence. "Hey, now that your dad is out, I was wondering if you could... uh... maybe tell me about you and Matthew?"

My heartbeat rises. It's not like she's asked me before if I've ever been seeing someone. Heck, when I came home after Kylie Monroe's party, mom could tell that something happened. I didn't mention her that I kissed

Nora, but I'm pretty sure that if I did, she would've been making such a huge fuss about it. "Are you sure you wanna know?" I ask her.

My mom nods. "Positive."

Oddly enough, I smile.

21

Apparently, neither my dad nor Matthew's parents can keep their mouths shut because when I get to school, everyone has definitely heard about us.

When I get to school on Monday, everyone—and I mean *everyone*—has heard about Matthew and I. Students turn their heads and watch me as they whisper amongst themselves. Some of them come forward and say a few comments, some, good, and some bad. At least three people judge me as I cross the hallways while many others show some support. The teachers are the same situation, except the ones who aren't so accepting judge me with disapproving glances instead of words. The ones that are more open try to cheer me up and tell me that they're here for me if I need to talk about something, but I don't want to talk to anybody. I just want to see Matthew.

I haven't spotted him anywhere around school yet and I couldn't get him on the phone. I sent a few texts but nothing, not even a damn read receipt. Maybe he isn't coming today. Maybe his parents didn't want him to be near me or even in the same classroom. God only knows what they must be saying to him.

When it's time for homeroom, I seat myself in the back of the room by the corner and bury my head in my palms. I feel others are watching me and I bury my head even harder. I want to disappear, fully. I want this to go away. Let me go back in the closet and spend a little extra time in there. It's not good for me, but at least it doesn't bring any of the problems I have now.

It's only around halfway through homeroom that Matthew walks into the classroom, and… Oh God, his eye! It's black and all swollen up. The bruising surrounds the entirety of his blue eye, and I can barely even see it. Did his dad hit him? It had to be him. Who else would've?

I confront him about it during snack period. We're sitting in the hallway when I ask him, to which he replies, "He… he hit me."

Anger boils inside me, more to my dad than his. Of

course, my dad would tell his. Why else wouldn't he? I cool myself down and address the current situation. "Are you okay?" I ask stroking his cheek.

"Not… really."

It's only then that I see a group of kids watching from not too far. I tell Matthew about it, and we walk into an empty classroom. I lock the door just for safe-keeping and lower the window curtains.

Once we're alone, Matthew breaks apart. He begins to sob, and tears begin to stream down his face. Seeing this, I pull him into a hug and caress his back gently. "It's okay," I whisper into his ear. "It's okay." I let him cry on my shoulder. If it were me, he would've done the same thing.

When he's let it all out, I grab him a paper towel and let him dry his cheeks. He blows his nose a little bit then throws it away before cleaning his hands with some hand sanitizer. "What did your dad do to you?" he asks me.

I scratch the back of my head. "Not much. He kept his cool but forced me into my room, and then my mom kicked him out."

Matthew smiles weakly. "You're lucky. When I got home both of my parents were disappointed with me.

Dad hit me, mom cried, and before I knew it, they were passing the blame on each other, on me, and then on to you. I…" His voice falters and a tear comes out of his swollen eye. "I tried to calm them down, but they didn't care."

Matthew starts crying again and I hug him back, only this time, I'm crying as well. It seems to be the only thing we can do now. Our families know our secret and it destroyed everything. The truth set us free, but at a cost of destroying our realities. If we'd known that, we would've stayed in our closets a while longer.

We can't crawl back in if we wanted to. No one can forget what they've heard. From now on, everyone will look at us differently, maybe for a little while, but always differently. I take Matthew's hand and squeeze it gently. "I'm here for you," I tell him.

"I know," he says, but it doesn't sound the same. It doesn't sound affirmative.

It sounds broken.

"So, your mom really kicked your dad out?" Nora asks me.

We're sitting in the courtyard together along with Alex and Matthew. Nora has her legs crossed whilst we chow down our sandwiches. Alex is sitting on the bench going over some math problems he has due for last period, but he's still listening to the conversation. Matthew is sitting right beside him. His head is lowered as he studies his swollen eye through his phone screen. I'm really worried about him. He hasn't said anything since we sat down, he's barely touched his lunch, and he looks like he's just… not here, in this moment.

"Hello," Nora says.

"What?" I ask. "Oh, yeah. She threw him out, and now he's staying in the motel just outside of town."

"Yikes," Nora says. "So, does that mean that you're not going to be sent to conversion therapy?"

"I hope so." My eyes fall on Matthew for a second. He still looks out of it. "Anyway, I didn't see you guys after the bonfire party. What did you and Alex do?"

We keep talking and thankfully, the topic of me and Matthew doesn't come back up. When lunch ends, we pick our stuff up and go our separate ways. I try to focus on my last two classes, but I keep thinking about Matthew and how silent he was. I don't know why, but something told me that he got more than just a beating and a broken heart. Maybe he got something worse. I could feel it when he told me what happened. He left something out, something big, and that something worries him as much as it worries me.

When school ends, I look for him around the hallways, and find him by the front of the school. I walk over and sit next to him. "Hey," I say.

"Hey," he says back.

"Do you have any plans after school?"

Matthew shakes his head. "I can't hang out, at least for now."

He sounds timid, fearful, and so... not him. "I see."

"But I'll call you," he says. "Tonight, when my parents are asleep."

I nod and give him a hug. Around a minute later, a car rolls up into the rotunda and I'm surprised to see Matthew's father in the driver's seat. What is he doing here? He never picks Matthew up. Then again, his secret just came out and he's not exactly open about it. I should probably leave before he sees me. Nope, too late.

Marcus spots Matthew sitting and then turns to see me. A shiver runs through my spine when I feel a cold stare coming from him. He is definitely angry, but with whom? Is he angry with me or is he angry with Matthew? Or is it both at the same time? It's most likely both of us. Seeing us together can do that.

"I have to go," Matthew says. "I'll call you."

"Cool," I say and watch as he goes. He jumps into the car and drives off faster than normal. His dad is pissed, really, *really* pissed. Whatever it is he'll do to Matthew is going to only make things worse. That beating seemed to have hit him harder than expected.

But there's something else that hit him as well. I feel it. Apart from the beating and crying, he got something else when he came home yesterday. A threat, maybe. I'm not sure. Whatever it is, it made Matthew shut me out like that, and it kills me to think that he feels like he can't talk to me about it. I want to be there for him. Whether he likes it or not, I'll be there to protect him.

This I swear.

22

I'm welcomed home with the sounds of screaming coming from the kitchen. When I get there, I find mom yelling at the phone. "You are not gonna do that at all," she yells. A few seconds of silence. "Don't you dare even... Ugh!" She ends the call as she slams her phone on the kitchen counter.

She turns to me, and her eyes widen, which in turn, makes me worry. "What's going on?" I ask. "Who was that?"

My mom sighs. "*That* was your father," she said, "and *he* just confirmed that he finished filling out the paperwork to send you to the conversion clinic."

Now I panic. My body stiffens, my heartbeat rises, and I start sweating like crazy. "H- how?" I say.

"I don't know," she exclaims. This is as frightening to her as it is to me. "I just got the email that told me that he just did. Maybe he forged my signature or something. I don't know, but I do know is that you leave this weekend."

"*This weekend?*" My breathing goes out of control.

My mom comes over and hugs me tightly. "I won't let him do that to you. I'm gonna fight this. I'm going over there right now and deal with this. I'll be back soon."

It's at this point that I begin to feel some bile come up my throat. "But—"

"No buts. I'll be back soon. Don't go anywhere."

I nod at her and watch her go. The second the front door closes, I head to the sink and throw up. I'm screwed. I'm definitely, *definitely* screwed. There's no way she'll be able to turn this thing around. It'll take a miracle for that to happen and I'm positive that's not going to happen.

For the rest of the day, I pace around the house, thinking of some possible solution to this whole thing. Sadly, nothing comes to mind and so I head upstairs and search dad's file cabinets for whatever information I can find on the clinic's bylaws. Mostly what I dig up is the visitation rights and the course planning, but when it comes to knowing about the treatments and how to pull someone out of there, the information is vague and confusing. I put the papers back in place and lie down on the bed. My eyes fall on the ceiling and silently, I start praying for a miracle.

Halfway through my prayer, my phone rings and I pull it out of my pocket. Matthew's name hovers on the screen. "Hey," I say, trying to sound happy.

"Hey," he says back. "Did I catch you in a bad time?"

"No," I say. "What's up?"

"Listen, I wanted to say I'm sorry for today. I know I acted all distant or something and to be honest, I felt bad about it. It's just that I was dealing with some shit and didn't wanna bother you."

"Hey, it's okay. I get that some stuff is hard, but I'm here for that."

"I know," Matthew says. Something about the way he says it makes it sound like he's not so optimistic about it. I brush it off.

"Where are you right now?" I ask.

"I'm in my room. My parents are downstairs talking to my uncle." A minute of silence. "Listen, I need to tell you something, something important, and I need to tell you now because I might never get a chance to say it to you again."

A part of me panics but I say, "Okay" timidly.

Matthew begins. "I love you. I've loved you since the day we first met and not once have I stopped loving you. You're the first thing I think of when I wake up, and the last thing that comes to mind before I fall asleep. Others may come after you, but none could compare to you. You're one of a kind. That's what's special about you."

My eyes widen. Never in my life has anyone told me something like that. He loves me. He thinks I'm special and unique. I love him so much. There's no one else I'd rather be with than him. He's special.

"I love you, too," I say. "So damn much. I don't want to be with anyone else but you. You're the most beautiful boy I've ever seen. We'll get through this. I promise."

A few seconds of silence. "Well... uh... I think this is the part where I spill out the bad news," he says.

I gulp. "What are you talking about?"

Matthew hesitates. "You know how I said that my parents were downstairs talking to my uncle?"

"Yes?"

"Well, the truth is that they're planning to send me to live with him, in Brazil."

"What?" I exclaim.

"I know, I know I just found out. I'm leaving on Friday."

"*Friday?*"

"Yeah. He's already told my uncle everything and he's making the preparations for me to live with him. On Friday, I head to the airport." Matthew pauses. "I need to ask you something and please, answer me honestly."

"What is it?"

Matthew hesitates for a moment. "If I were to tell you that I was running away, would you come with me?"

I raise an eyebrow. "Are you actually planning on running away?"

Matthew takes a deep breath. "Yes. I don't want to go to live with my uncle, and I don't want to leave you, so that's why I'm asking."

"What about coming to stay with us? My mom kicked my dad out and she's pretty much open about our relationship. We have a guest room you can stay in.

We won't have to struggle. We could still stay."

"My parents will never just let me go. They'll come after me. When my dad sets his mind on something, he won't rest until he's finished."

I don't know what to say now. Matthew can't stay here because of his dad, and I can't stay here either because of my dad. Still, can I just do that? Can I just pack a bag, hitch a ride out of town and leave everyone I care about behind? Can it really be that simple?

"Where would we even go?" I ask.

"I don't know," he says. "All I know is that it has to be better than this. So, are you gonna come with me or not?"

I don't know if I'm going to regret this, but I love him too much to lose him. "Yes," I say.

23

Matthew tells me that he'll be at my house within thirty minutes and orders me to pack a bag. "Take whatever's necessary," he says. "Forget about any personal belongings. Just pack some supplies and some cash." The phone call ends before I can say anything and rather than pondering around what I just signed up for, I prep myself for when he arrives.

I go to my room, pick a backpack, and start stuffing in whatever I can find; canned goods that'll last us for a while, two full outfits, some cash, and a few signed baseballs dad has that we could sell at a pawn shop for a good price. I go into my dad's toolbox and pull out a pocketknife, for our safety, of course. I dig up a map and stuff it in the bag. If anything, we could head to the city. Maybe we can find the same people who helped

Kyle and figure out our next steps from there.

A part of me thinks this whole thing is crazy. I mean, how am I supposed to fend for myself on the street when I don't even know what to do first? Well, obviously, first things first is to get as far from here as we possibly can. After that, we'll find some place to camp down for the night and then take it day by day. Sounds simple, if you forget how you need to pick from the trash, sleep in the outdoors and not shower because you don't have the luxury of warm food, a soft bed and a shower. I'm definitely not equipped for this. But it looks like I don't have a choice.

I head downstairs and pick up a paper and a pencil, then proceed downstairs to write a note for my mom. It doesn't take that much time. I just explain to her that I'll be running off with Matthew, blah, blah, blah, and I make sure to let her know that I'll call her once I'm somewhere safe. After that, I race upstairs and leave the note on her nightstand. A part of me hates this part, but it's the best I can do. It'll be harder for her than it'll be for me, but she'll get through this. I know she can.

When I finish packing up a bag, I text Matthew to see if he's on his way. For the next five minutes, I stare at the screen waiting for a response. But not even a read receipt comes flying in. I can only think of two reasons why: either he got caught by his parents or he left his phone. I pray that it's the latter.

It's only then that I hear the garage door open and a car roll in. My heartbeat rises. When the engine shuts off, I hear my mom call my name. *Shit*, I think. This is going to be harder than it was already going to be.

Do I run away? Maybe I should. If I stay, she might ask about the bag or why Matthew is at our front lawn when he gets here. But where will I go? Matthew's picking me up here and he still hasn't replied back.

The doorknob shifts. My mom walks in. She looks at me with the bag in my shoulder and my heart jumps out. "Oh, honey," she says. "You're awake."

I raise an eyebrow. "It's only 7:15," I say. I notice the worried look on her face. "Is something wrong?"

She shakes her head. "No. Nothing's wrong."

She's lying. I can tell. I eye her sternly.

My mom takes a deep breath. "I went to the clinic and there's nothing I can do that'll keep them from getting you committed."

I gulp. Well, at least I have a reason to run away.

"I can lawyer up," she says. "But it's going to take some time to handle. Unless your father calls it off, the only thing I can do is hide you somewhere."

My eyes widen. I think I have a crazy idea. "Then let's do it," I say.

"What?"

"I said that we should do it. Hide me. Hide *us*."

I spend the better part of ten minutes trying to explain to my mom as much of my crazy plan as possible. When I finished, she looked at me like I was crazy. Then she said, "Alright. We'll do it. But what makes you think Matthew would tag along with this?"

"Matthew's parents are planning on sending him to live in Brazil with his uncle. He can either join in on this or go to South America, the latter of which I know he'll never do."

That seems to convince mom, and so she makes the preparations. She makes some calls, packs some stuff up, and preps things up. When it's all ready, we wait for Matthew to arrive. He rolls in ten minutes after that, hopped on his father's motorcycle. A backpack hangs from his shoulders. When he sees me and my mom waiting for him, he looks stunned. "What's going on?" he asks.

I smile. "Come inside and I'll explain everything."

I tell him all the details, and after that, Matthew joins in on this. With that settled, Matthew and I hop on the motorcycle and follow my mom. We drive out of town and into the city where we head to the motel where my mom made the reservation. When we get to the front desk, my mom pays in cash and is handed the keys. The man at the front desk didn't look at us suspiciously or anything. He did, on the other hand, take a close look at Matthew and me and noticed that we couldn't be biologically related.

Our room is—in my opinion—cozy-ish. Two beds lie pressed to the wall separated by one nightstand with a lamp in the center. A dresser stands in front of the beds with a television on top of it. There's a minifridge to the side along with a small counter holding a coffee maker. The closet is to the back, and in front of it lies the door that leads to the bathroom.

At first, I thought it was alright, but when I look closely with the lights on, I can see the crappiness of the place. The gray walls have stains as do the carpets. The sheets of the bed have holes in them and for some reason they itch a little. Thankfully, the bathroom isn't that bad, but the packed soap is definitely old. I sigh. I don't have anywhere else to go. This is the cheapest motel mom could find and it's where Matthew and I are going to be staying for a while.

Once we're in the room, mom closes the door and shuts the curtains. Then she sets down the rules. "You guys are gonna be sleeping here for I don't know how long while I work on figuring out how to keep you guys safe." She points to Matthew. "I'm not sure if keeping you here is illegal or something, but I better hope it isn't. I didn't exactly kidnap you, so at least I don't have to worry about getting arrested for that. You two stay here, and for God's sake don't do anything stupid."

Matthew and I nod. My mom tells us that she's going to run to the bank for a while and orders us to stay here until she returns. When she leaves, the tension inside me ceases. I exhale in relief and bury my head in my palms. Everything was just hitting me. We were actually doing this when like not that long ago, this whole thing seemed crazy. Yet, here I am, in a motel in the city, with my boyfriend, hiding from his parents and my dad.

Matthew doesn't seem to react the same way I do. I guess he's handling it better than I am. "Everything's going to be alright," he says.

For some odd reason, I believe him. It's crazy but

I do. When I look into his eyes, I see the spark that he lost when it all came out in the open. Now it was back, stronger, clearer, and better than ever, confident that in the end, everything would work out. I smile, and Matthew smiles back, then proceeds to put his arm around me. I lay my head on his shoulder and close my eyes. I can never resist the security he offers me, and I never want to.

Because that security—he saves it all for me.

24

Despite the itchy sheets, I was able to get a good night sleep. I felt partially uncomfortable, but I didn't get any rashes, and thankfully, I was able to sleep peacefully. I credit that to how exhausted I was from the drive to get here, but I also have to credit Matthew for that.

Instead of he and I sleeping in separate beds, Matthew crawled into mine when he saw me struggling with the sheets. I did nothing to stop him—if anything, I moved aside so that he could jump in. The bed wasn't that big, so we had to cuddle so neither of us fell to the floor. He wrapped his arms around me, and I wrapped my arms around them. Something about him holding me the way he did make the rest of the stuff we'd done seem incompatible. Maybe it was when he caressed me or when his body heat engulfed me. Cuddling with him made me feel closer to him than ever before, and to me, that was all I ever wanted, to be close to him here until the end of time.

When morning comes, I wake up still wrapped up in Matthew's arms. Sunlight pours through the window curtain, hitting the wall in front of me. I can hear the sound of cars honking and engines running from outside. Matthew is still asleep. I can hear him snoring lightly. The sound is so sweet that it makes me smile.

I take his arms off me, carefully avoiding any movement that would wake him up. Once free, I pick a fresh pair of clothes and head into the bathroom. I strip, shower, and get dressed. I come out of the bathroom as I finish putting my shirt on. Matthew is already up, dressed in jeans and sneakers. His shirt is in his hands. I avoid staring for too long.

"You don't need to worry," Matthew says. "You've already seen me naked so seeing me shirtless can't be that bad."

Without any restraint, I look back at him. I study the lines and physique of his muscles, lean, and perfectly cut. My chest fires up. I've seen him before, when we were together in his room for the second time. But I haven't seen it like this, with the opportunity to admire it, admire him. Matthew smiles. "You really like what you see, don't you?"

I blush. Matthew laughs. "I'll take that as a yes." A few seconds of silence. "We should probably go find some breakfast."

I nod and let him get dressed. Thirty minutes after that, the two of us are at a diner three blocks from the motel. We order plain dishes, eggs for him and pancakes for me. The waitress that brings it to us smiles when she sees us together. Then her expression changes at the sight of Matthew's black eye. By now, it was less swollen, and most of the bruising had gone away, but it was still noticeable. She doesn't ask him about it, but he took notice of her expression, and he lowers his head.

It's only then that I see him holding back something. It's not tears, but something deeper, something that not even all the crying and screaming can express. Maybe it's pain. Maybe his parents' reaction hit him harder than I thought. I know the feeling and I fear asking him about it. I worry it might break him. Instead, I say, "How's the eye doing?"

Matthew looks up. "Good. Still a little sore, but good."

I take a chance. "And how are *you* doing?"

Matthew's expression changes. "Honestly, okay-ish."

"*Ish?*" Immediately, I regret it.

"It's nothing," he says. "It's just the whole coming out thing wasn't something I was prepared for. I kinda wish I could've had more time."

Matthew places his hands on the table. His head looks down at them and he watches as he picks a nail. I could see the sadness written in his eyes. He's broken, really broken, maybe more than I thought he was. A parent's rejection would do that to anybody.

I lift a hand and grab a hold of his. I wrap my fingers around his and squeeze it gently. "It's okay," I say. "We're in this together. Whatever you need, I'll be here."

Matthew looks up at me and smiles. I smile back. I've put a temporary band aid on him, but I'm hopeful that he won't be needing it for that long.

Later in the afternoon when Matthew is out, I text Nora.

> **Me:** Hey. You free to talk?
> **Nora:** Sure. You wanna keep texting or do a
> phone call.

Me: Phone call.

Nora calls me within a few seconds. I answer it. "Hey," I say.

"Hey," she says back. "Where are you? I didn't see you in school today."

"I'm in a motel in the city, hiding from my dad. Long story."

"Yeah, I know. Your mom told me and Alex."

"Really?"

"Yeah. She told us how your dad signed the clinic papers and how it was all your idea to go hide off in the city. Is Matthew with you?"

"He's out, but he'll be back soon. Anyway, yeah. It was my idea. It beats living out on the streets."

"So, you and Matthew were going to run away?"

"Yeah. Lucky for us that my mom decided to help us."

"Well, you might wanna get comfortable there. Your mom is working on keeping you out of that hell-hole, but it might take some time. As for Matthew, his parents are still angry and disappointed in him."

"How are Matthew's parents?"

"How do you think they'd be when their only son

ran away? Worst part is that they blame you for it. Something between the lines of you and the 'Devil's influence.'"

"So, I'll take that as a sign that they haven't done anything yet."

"Well, they went to your house to look for him and your mom said that he wasn't there, and neither were you. She denied knowing where you two were, but Marcus and your dad are working on finding you both."

"Do they have any leads?"

"Not that I know of. I tried getting something out of them, but they just told me not to worry about it. I did talk to Matthew's mom, and so did your mom."

"What did you say?"

"I told her how she had one job with raising Matthew and she failed at it. I also said that if she really loves Matthew, she'd appreciate him for who he is."

"What did she say to that?"

"She said that it was sinful to side with the Devil and whatnot. I think she would've slapped me if she could, but then she'd have to deal with my parents, so she didn't. My mom talked to her, and so did yours. I don't know what they said. All I know is that the next time I saw her, she was a bit more chill regarding the topic of you guys."

"Really?"

"Yeah. My mom's good friends with her. She pulled some hard lengths, but she got through to her. And your mom really cares about you. She's sacrificing a lot for you two. Most of her friends support her or turn her away. She was lucky to get any of the lawyers in town to take her case."

"Who's representing my mom?"

"I don't know. I'll figure that out later. But enough about you and Matthew's parents. How are you guys?

"We're as comfortable as we can be. I'm honestly more worried about Matthew."

"Did something happen?"

"Not exactly, but he does seem… broken, in a way. I think it's because of how his parents reacted when they found out he was gay." A moment of silence. "I just wish I could help him somehow."

"You are. You're being there for him. That's enough."

"But he doesn't seem to be getting better."

"Well, you need to give him time. Remember how you were the first few days when you came out to them? You weren't exactly sunshine and rainbows. The only reason you recovered so soon was because you fell in love with him. He's probably getting it rougher than you. He's probably having it worse since he was forced to run away from home and beaten by his father. Just be there for him, and everything will work out."

"Okay." I hear footsteps coming closer to the door. "I gotta go."

"One more thing," Nora says. "If we ever get the chance, can Alex and I come visit you?"

"Sure. Just make sure you have a good cover." The door opens. Matthew steps inside. "See you later."

"Bye." The phone call ends.

"Who were you talking to?" Matthew asks.

I look at him. "Nora."

"Did she say anything important?"

"Apart from what my mom's doing to keep us safe from our dads, she told us we might wanna make ourselves comfortable."

"What are our dads doing?"

I tell him everything, from my mom getting a lawyer to our dads planning to file a missing person's reports on us. By the time I finish, Matthew's jaw is hanging down. "Shit," he says.

"Yeah, that pretty much describes it. We're gonna

be here a while." I notice Matthew has a worried face. "Don't worry about it. They're not gonna win."

"How would you know," he asks.

I smile. "Because I have faith," I say, which is something I've learned to have.

25

I'll admit that from the moment I set this plan in motion, I knew that Matthew and I were walking on thin ice. We managed to buy ourselves some time, but it's not going to last forever. Sooner or later Matthew's dad and mine will find some clues as to where we are. Either they'll squeal it out of my mom, or they'll get it some other way. My mom promises to keep her mouth shut for as long as she can.

I can only hope that nothing goes wrong.

On Tuesday morning, my mom drops in again to bring us some spending cash–a thousand bucks in total. Where she got it, I don't know, but what I do know is that she tells us to go out into the city. "I know keeping you here all day is most likely torture, so I might as well give you some spending money," she says. "Have fun and don't spend it all at once." Matthew and I nod at her, and she leaves after promising to bring more cash in a few days.

After that, Matthew and I talk about how to make the money last. We choose to make a daily budget of a hundred bucks a day and not spend any more than that. If we stick to it, we'll have enough money for ten days. My mom is still working on the legal issues to keep me out of the conversion clinic, and Nora and Alex are trying to get Matthew's parents to change their minds about sending Matthew away. Nora texts me early in the day to say that she thinks she's getting through to his mom, but his dad is more difficult. "I think it'll take a miracle for him to change his mind," she says in a phone call. I tell her to keep trying and that I miss her before I end the call.

Matthew seems to be feeling a little better than yesterday. He looks like his head is less deep in the clouds and he doesn't seem so down. He's still hurting, but he's getting better, and that's a start.

Since we have the whole day for ourselves, Matthew and I decide to go around town in search of something to do. With a hundred bucks in our pockets, we end up in this little market where we spend a few days going through each of the stands. We end up spending half the money on some snacks, drinks, and this brown leather journal that I bought for Matthew after it caught his attention. Matthew said that I didn't have to, but I told him that I know that he'll put it to good use. "I'm not sure what to do with it," he says.

"Whatever you want," I tell him. I don't give him any ideas. Whatever he does with it has to come from him.

That night, Matthew surprises me with dinner from the diner where we had breakfast on our first day here. "You bought me that journal, so this is my way of paying you back," he said. I give him a kiss and whisper a thank you into his ear.

We sit on the floor as we eat. Matthew scrolls through the television channels until he finds us a good movie to watch. It's a comedy, and if I may add, it literally killed me. Almost twice did I choke on my own food because of a funny scene, and a moment came where I accidentally spat soda on Matthew because of the last joke. "Sorry," I say.

Matthew wipes some soda from his cheek. "It's

okay," he says. "Glad to see you enjoyed it."

We clean up and throw the food out in the trash can. After which, I excuse myself to go to the bathroom where I shower and readied myself for bed. When I come out, I see Matthew writing something in the leather journal I bought him. I smile. "What are you writing in there?" I ask.

Matthew looks up at me smiles. "Nothing important," he says, closing the book.

I can tell that he's lying, but it's his journal, not mine. Whatever he writes in there is for his eyes only. He puts the journal away and goes to take a shower. I'm almost tempted to sneak a peek in it, but instead, I pass the time by searching for our next activity for tomorrow. Matthew comes out of the bathroom dressed in shorts and a tank top. I look at him and smile. "You look good," I say.

Matthew blushes and blows me a kiss. "Let's get some shut eye," he says, and we shut the lights off and go to sleep.

On Thursday afternoon, we get a surprise visit from Nora and Alex. Mom pulls up in her car and my smile widens when I see Nora and Alex stepping out of the backseat. Matthew and I are greeted with warm hugs from both of them. My mom says that she'll be back in two hours to take them back home. "Stay out of trouble," she tells us, and she takes off.

Nora fills us in on what's been going on with our parents. "Your mom got herself a lawyer as you already know, and she's already building up a case to go against your dad. The divorce might help. If she wins custody over you, your dad's signature on that paper might not be worth anything. Your dad is completely stressed, with the divorce and looking for you." She turns to Matthew. "Your dad is stressed about you as well."

"Have they done anything to try and find us?" Matthew asks.

"They filed a missing person's report," Alex says, "but it might not lead them anywhere. There aren't any clues as to where you went and so far, they're only looking for you guys in the nearby towns. Still, I think sooner or later they might call off the search."

"Why is that?"

Nora and Alex look at each other. "The townspeople have been splitting up.," Nora says. "Some are siding with your dad's, and some are siding with Taylor's mom. Some people haven't chosen a side, and it looks as if the town council will have a debate regarding the search."

"But they can't do anything to protect us?" I ask.

She shakes her head. "The council members aren't your parents. The only way this is sorted out is through your parents." She points a finger to me. "In your case, it'll be by who gets custody over you."

I look at Matthew and then look at Nora. "How's the divorce going, by the way?"

Nora bites her lip. "Well, neither your dad nor your mom are taking it well, but your dad has it worse. Your mom's been breathing down his neck and he's got a lot on his plate. If he breaks down, the court might hand your custody to your mom."

"And what about my parents?" Matthew asks.

Alex replies. "Your dad is… well, the same. Your mom, on the other hand, has been thinking about what Nora said and she might be close to siding with Taylor's mom."

"Really?" I say astonished.

"Yeah, really. It's crazy but it's the truth. She's not divorcing your dad, but she's starting to think that the problem isn't you, but them."

We keep talking and after a while, my mom comes

back. We say our goodbyes and promise to meet again next week. When they drive off, Matthew goes back inside. I follow him from behind. "Something on your mind?" I ask.

Matthew shakes his head. "Nah. How 'bout you?"

I bite my lip. "I'm just wondering how this is all going to end."

He places a hand over my shoulder. "It's all going to be okay," he says.

I roll my eyes. "I'm getting tired of hearing that."

Matthew laughs. "Then here's something different," he says, and gives me a kiss.

Friday night, Matthew and I go exploring and we end up at this steakhouse where they served us these steaks that took up three fourths of the space on the plate. I grab a bite and... Oh my God! Super good! I end up eating it all in under ten minutes. Matthew looks at me the same way when he saw me eating pizza. Suddenly, and idea hits me. "You feel like dancing?" I ask.

Matthew reads between the lines and gets where I'm going with it. "Yes," he says.

An hour later, we reach the alley where the entrance to the club is at. A different bouncer waits for us there.

Matthew gives the password and before I know it, we're dancing in the basement together. He wraps his arms around me as a pop song bursts out through the speakers. We dance for a while, until I'm too tired to keep at it. We make our way to a booth where we rest for a while. After which, I excuse myself to get us some drinks.

I come back with two waters with a splash of booze. We drink them slowly, and when we finish, Matthew pulls me into a kiss. "What was that?" I ask when he pulls away.

Matthew giggles. "What? I can't kiss you?"

I lean a little closer. "You can kiss me anytime," I whisper.

I don't know what happens after that, but I do know is that we make our way into the motel room with our lips together and our hands on each other. We come crashing down into the nearest bed where we take our clothes off and get under the sheets. For a long time, we have fun, and when we're done, we cuddle up and stay like that. Matthew falls asleep first, snoring lightly and with his head next to mine. I watch him for a while. He looks so peaceful next to me. Carefully, I kiss his cheek and then close my eyes and fall into a deep sleep.

The next morning, I wake up to the sound of my phone ringing. The sun is barely up, and the city lights are still lit up in the darkness. A fogginess of rain is coming from the outside. I turn my head and look at Matthew. He's still sleeping, but the ringing is waking him up.

"Who was it?" he asks hoarsely.

By now, the phone has stopped ringing and I pick it up to see who it was.

It was my mom calling, and before that, she'd called four times in the night. That's when a message pops up.

Mom: Emergency! Answer the phone!

Matthew's falling back to sleep as I slip out of bed and head to the bathroom. I shut the door and dial my mom. "Hello," I say.

"Oh, thank God," she exclaims relieved. "I was worried sick! Whey weren't you answering your phone?"

I yawn. "Mom, you do realize that it's an hour before morning?"

"Are you still at the motel?" She sounds worried, which makes me worried.

"Yeah. Why?"

"Listen to me. You and Matthew need to get out of there, now."

"Wait, why? Also, why do you sound like this is life or death?"

"Because…" Her voice falters. Something in my gut tells me that this isn't something good. Why else would she call me so early in the day? It certainly isn't to check on us. My palms fill with sweat, and my heartbeat rises. I pray that this is all just in my head.

It isn't.

"Your father is on his way," my mom says. "He knows where you two are and he's got company."

26

Mom doesn't wait for me to ask her how he knows to tell me that she has no idea. "He must've followed me there or something," she said. "I only found out because he confronted me about how I've been lying to him and how he knows where you are. I tried to deny it, but he told me to save it and that he was heading there now. Matthew's father is tagging along with him, as are some people from the clinic. They'll be there in half an hour. You need to leave, now."

"But—"

"No buts," she intervenes. I can hear the panic in her voice. "You need to disappear. Pack what you can and get as far away from the motel as you can. Call me when you're somewhere safe and I'll meet you there. We'll figure out what to do next later. For now, you both need to disappear."

"Mom—"

"I'm on my way over there. Stay safe."

"But wait. Where—"

The phone call ends. "Fuck," I yell out. My hands shake, and my heart pounds. I need to get out of here. *Matthew* and I need to get out of here, now.

A knock comes from the door and Matthew pops into the bathroom. He sees my worried face, which makes him worry. "Is something wrong?" he asks.

I nod and explain our situation. "Shit," he says when I finish. "Well… we better get going then."

We don't waste any time. Matthew and I get dressed and start packing up whatever cash and clothes we can. We stuff it all in one backpack and zip it shut. I hoist the backpack in my shoulders just as Matthew comes over to me with the leather journal in his hands. "Think there's room for it?" he asks.

Honestly, we're at near capacity, but I take the backpack off my shoulders and say, "Sure," before I proceed to stuff the journal inside with all my strength. "You ready?"

"Yeah," he says. "Let's get out of here."

Suddenly, I hear the sound of engines rolling in and

shutting off in front of the motel. My heartbeat accelerates. I walk over to the window and ever so fearfully lift the curtain gently for a peek. Outside are three plain white vans with blacked out windows. Two men pop out of each van, some even carrying what look like tranquilizer dart guns. A fourth car parks in front of the office building, a regular black Lexus. I recognize it immediately: it's my dad's car.

A yelp escapes from my lips. I hide behind the curtains again. Matthew is standing behind me, panic already writing itself on his face. It's a good thing we have an escape plan. "The back window," I say.

Matthew and I quickly head towards the back of the room where we gently open the window and climb out the alley. Not much fills it except a couple of trash bins and some backdoors. A dead end is on one side, and the other is the only way out. To the dead end lies Marcus's motorcycle hidden by a bunch of trash bags. We'll be making noise when that thing turns on, but hopefully, we'll be out of sight by the time they could make their way over here.

Matthew goes out the window first and runs to get the motorcycle. I follow right behind him. Once I'm outside, I slide the window down and get out of sight.

Matthew rolls the bike over to me, and once he's near, he tells me to hop on. I get on the back and wrap my arms around his stomach. This scene is familiar to me; the time he and I first came into the city, the night I felt freer than ever before. "Ready to go?" he asks.

I hear a knock coming from a door. Our door. "Yes," I say.

Matthew starts the engine, and we drive off.

The good news is that they weren't on our tail for the first few blocks. The bad news is that they weren't on our tail for the first few blocks.

I don't know how they found us, but all I know is that just as we were driving through an intersection, I spotted one of the white vans driving by and not five seconds later do I hear them call our names out, followed by an order for us to pull over. I tap Matthew on the shoulder and tell him to step on it just as the light turns green. The van follows us from behind, continuing to yell at us to stop and how they "just want to help."

"Don't stop," I yell to Matthew.

"Got it," he says, and he increases the speed.

Matthew takes a turn that leads us out of the city.

From there, we dive into a backroad that gets a lot more off-road by the mile. The van is still following us, and it's already been joined by the others. I spot my dad's car among them. I can feel his angry cold stare from afar. Goosebumps go through me. I turn my focus back to the road ahead.

Thankfully, the motorcycle can handle the increase in the off-road conditions, but the vans and my dad's car cannot. I saw it every time I turned around. The vans and my dad were falling behind by the mile. After a moment, they're out of sight, and I exhale in relief. They're still onto us, but we'll lose them soon. We just have to find someplace safe.

"Where to now?" Matthew asks.

I look at the surrounding trees. "I'm not sure," I say. "Just keep going forward and we'll see where we can stop."

"Alright."

We ride for a while, and thankfully, we reach an intersection that splits into three different roads. Two of them lead to nearby small towns while the other leads to a town further away. I don't bother with the log-ic or anything. I tell Matthew to take the road that'll lead us to the furthest of the towns. Maybe it was a mistake. The road was even more rough than the other ones, and the motorcycle could barely handle it. Either way, I kept telling Matthew to keep going because if we turned around, we might confront them.

That was an even bigger mistake. Just as we were crossing a bridge, the front wheel dives into a pothole and we go crashing to the ground. The good news is that neither I nor Matthew are that badly hurt. We only end up with some scratches, a few rashes, and some bruises. The bad news is that the bike was put out of commission just like that. I don't how it happened, but I knew it was done for the second I saw fuel leaking out of it. The wheel partially busted too. I curse under my breath.

"What now?" Matthew asks.

I pull my phone out to call my mom. No service. I curse again. I put the phone away and stand up. "I guess we're walking," I say. I don't like the idea of us hitchhiking in the woods alone, but we don't have a choice. I just hope that the town isn't that far.

I take the bike and hide it under the trees. If anyone comes rolling by, they won't see it, which is exactly what we need when it comes to keeping a low profile. I hoist my backpack onto my shoulders and get walking. Matthew walks next to me, hiking along the trail in broad daylight. It was fine at first, but then my feet started to hurt, and I started taking breaks to let the pain die down. Matthew would do the same, and when either of us stopped to rest, the other would go forward a bit to see if there was at least a gas station up front. But in all the times we did it, we didn't find even a road sign that told us where we were heading.

Then came the rain. Walking in the middle of nowhere gets worse when it starts to pour like a rain shower. Matthew and I went under the cover of the trees with the hope that the leaves would cover us. They did, a little bit, but we still got wet. The rain tore through the leaves and came down on us hard. Everything— even my underwear—gets wet. My body is freezing, and a constant wave of shivers keeps running through me.

Matthew and I find this little cave not too long after it started pouring where we hole up for a while. For two long hours, we stay in there, wrapped up to keep warm whilst our bodies shivered, and our teeth clattered like crazy. "How are you holding up?" Matthew asks me.

I give him a weak smile. "Fantastic," I say sarcastically.

We talk a bit, hoping to distract ourselves from the fact that we're freezing. It works for a while, but it's hard to keep the conversation going when you stutter through each word because your body's temperature is dropping by the minute. In my head, I pray that this ends quickly, and the sun comes out.

It stops raining a while later, and thankfully the sun pours out. Matthew and I slip out of the cave and keep walking, but it's not exactly easy. We're both soaking wet, tired, hungry, and totally, totally lost. My skin is cold and the hairs in my arms are standing perfectly straight. I'm freezing and the humidity isn't exactly doing anything in our favor.

I turn to Matthew, who's pace is slow, but simple. He's got his arms wrapped around his chest and he's also zipped up his hoodie. His blonde hair is wet, but it's mostly dried up, and the same goes for his clothes. Still, he's cold. No amount of walking and waiting will help us. We need towels, fresh sets of clothes and a fire. I just wish someone would drive by and pick us up.

No one comes, sadly, and things take a turn for the worse for us. My fingers start to feel numb, and so do my bones. My breaths become shallower, and the more time passes, the harder it gets to even feel my heartbeat.

Rubbing my hands together isn't helping anymore. All I can feel is cold skin against cold skin. My teeth clatter faster than ever, and my lips are cracking.

I press on. Maybe there's a stop up front that we can take shelter in. Maybe there isn't. There wasn't one in the past couple hours, there might not be one in the next couple of hours. "Maybe we should turn around," I suggest. "We could try and take shelter in some of the other towns."

Matthew licks his lip. "If we turn around, it'll take us longer to find shelter," he says. "It's best if we keep going forward."

"Forward," I say astonished.

"Yes," Matthew says. "Look."

Matthew points forward to a sign hidden by a tree shade. The sign tells the name of a town that's roughly eight miles away. "We'll never make it," I say.

"We will. You just gotta have faith."

I buy into his crazy and keep going forward. By now, my body is at its last lengths. Almost every muscle of mine is numb, and my feet are on the brink of breaking apart. I slow my pace to save some strength, but it only makes it last longer. Matthew takes notice and slows down to stay by my side. He unzips his hoodie and puts it over me. "I can't," I tell him. "You'll get cold."

"Doesn't matter," he says. "You look like you need it more than I do."

I don't have the energy to fight him, and to be honest, I want the hoodie badly. But despite having it on, I'm still cold, and my condition gets worse. I feel my blood circulation slow down, and my heartbeat decrease. My head starts to feel heavier, probably because of how dehydrated I am. My eyes start to tear up, and it only brings more pain.

Eventually, it all comes to an end, but not because I got better.

It was because my eyes rolled up and I crashed to the ground.

27

The good thing is that I'm not dead, at least not yet. I'm getting there, however, and it's not going smoothly.

My entire body feels like it's shutting down, turning into a cold lifeless shell by the minute. The last bit of warmth left in me is dying out or being used up to keep me alive for just a little while longer. I try my best to open my eyes, but my vision is super cloudy that I can barely see. I think Matthew is holding me. I can hear the vagueness of his voice hovering above. I feel him shake me, caress me, and do anything that would signal that I'm not dead yet. It takes all my strength to speak, but the words barely come out.

The world around me feels as if it's fading. Noises are becoming bleaker by the minute and my ability to be aware of anything is going away at the same pace. I try my best to fight it, but it's hopeless. It's ending for me. I can feel it. The last bit of life left in me is already dying out. I'm starting to lose control of myself, and I can't even feel parts of me.

I always knew Matthew and I wouldn't make it this far, only because I looked at the worst-case scenario of it all. But a part of me still imagined what our lives would be like if things worked out. Maybe we would've gone back home after all of this was sorted out. Maybe we'd be able to live out our lives together. Maybe we wouldn't be in this situation.

Guess it was all just wishful thinking.

Bits of white light hover over my vision. I try to fight them, but they keep getting brighter. My heart-beat accelerates. I'm not sure if it'll make the situation worse, but I'm not stupid. I know what they mean, and I'm certainly not ready yet. But no one's ever ready when they're as young as I am. I still have so much to live for, so much I haven't yet done. Yet, here I am, lost in the woods, dying of hypothermia, in my boyfriend's arms with no chance of making it out.

Matthew still hovers over me, and I think I can hear him crying and sobbing. I feel the delicate touch of teardrops landing on my cheeks. They're ice cold on my skin. It takes all my remaining strength to lift a hand up in search of Matthew's face. When I find his cheek, I use it to wipe away his tears. "I love you," I whisper because that's all I'm capable of doing.

Matthew sniffs. "I love you too," I hear him say. My lips curve into a smile. I don't want to die, but I have to admit, dying in his arms was something I dreamed of happening. I just wish it could've been after we've lived a long life together.

Matthew takes my hand and squeezes it gently. I can barely feel the warmth of his skin. Still, I do my best to wrap my fingers around his. He proceeds to hoist my body over to his and wraps me in an embrace. A wave of heat engulfs me, handing me a small amount that'll buy me some more time. "I've got you," he says. "I won't let you go."

I'll keep fighting, for his sake as well as mine. I may not have the strength anymore, but I still have some bit of life left. I'm not going to lie around and let it wither.

I wrap an arm around him, and I cling on to him with all my will.

I think I must've passed out because as soon as I cling on to him, I closed my eyes and then woke up to the sound of an engine running and to the blinding light of a headlight on my face. I turn my head to avoid the light, but either way, I smile. Someone found us. Someone *actually* found us. Maybe there's still a chance for me.

Someone hoists me up from the ground and gets me into the backseat of a car. Once I'm there, I feel a soft blanket being placed over me. Immediately, the blanket gets to work on warming me up. I cover myself with it and let the feeling sink in. It takes a bit of time for my body to stop shivering so much, and a while after that, I start to warm up.

When I open my eyes again, I get a vague view of my surroundings. I'm still in the car, driving quickly through the woods. Matthew is seated next to me, with my head resting on his lap. He keeps working on warming me up, and thankfully, it helps a lot. There are two people seated up front. Based on their voices, they're a man and a woman. They ask Matthew a bunch of questions, and he answers them, vaguely, which makes me glad because I'm not sure what they'll do if they knew the full story.

I finally get the strength to say something. "Matthew," I say weakly.

Matthew strokes my cheek. "Hush now," he says gently. "It's okay. We're almost there."

I'm tempted to ask where we're going, but my eyes roll up and I pass out again.

I'm barely conscious the next time I open my eyes. All I know is that I'm probably being rolled by a hallway. I can feel my body lying on a flat surface, the warmth of ceiling lights hovering above me. A few people linger around me. I can't make out their appearances, but I do get the clarity of a few voices.

"Talk to me," a man says.

A woman replies. "Patient is a teenage boy, seventeen years of age, suffering from an extreme case of hypothermia. Loss of consciousness and slurred speech already in effect."

"Alright," the man replies. "Let's get to work."

My eyes roll up again, and I wake up sometime later in a bed. The walls and floor are plain white and there's nothing hanging on the walls except a television. To my side lies a nightstand along with a few machines that make sounds and beeps. A small window gives out a view of the night. I look down at my body. I'm covered in a series of blankets, and I can tell that I'm no longer wearing my wet clothes. My body feels warmer, less stiff, and honestly, really weak.

"Matthew," I call as I get up. My voice is still weak.

Matthew appears from the side. "Hey," he says as he gently pulls me back to bed. "Lie down. You need your rest."

"Where… Where are we?"

"We're in a hospital in the outskirts of the city. How are you feeling?"

I grunt. "Tired. How long have we been here?"

"A couple of hours." A few seconds of silence. "Your mom is on her way, and so is your dad."

I struggle with widening my eyes. "My *dad*?"

"Relax. He's not taking us. He just wants to talk." He studies my face. "You're tired. Get some rest while you can. We'll talk later."

Matthew raises the blanket a little, and despite me not wanting to rest, I close my eyes.

When I wake up again, the sun has already risen. My body no longer felt cold, and I could feel my body completely. My strength is back and I'm fully aware of my surroundings.

Matthew is standing over me, as is my mom. When she notices me waking up, she starts to cry. "Baby," she says, pressing a hand to my cheek. "Are you okay? How are you feeling?"

I sit myself straight. "Better," I say weakly. I look at Matthew and study his tired face. Then I remember what he's said. "Is dad—"

"He's outside," she says. "Don't worry. He wants to speak to you."

A part of me wants to laugh, but I don't when I realize that she's not lying. I tell her to let him come and she and Matthew excuse themselves the moment he comes in. There's a jolt of fear coming through me when the door closes behind them. Me and my dad haven't had a conversation since he found out I was dating Matthew, and he wasn't at all okay with it. After all this, God only knows what he must be thinking.

But then I think of how they told me that he just wants to talk, and when I look into his eyes, I can see that something's changed. There's no anger written over them.

All I see is just… guilt.

"Taylor," he says. His voice sounds shaky. "I'm… I'm sorry." Tears start to cloud his eyes as he takes my hand into his. "I'm so, so sorry."

Eventually, he pulls it together enough to be able

to explain himself. Apparently, losing his only son was more painful to him than who I dated, and when he heard about my near death, he started thinking, and then ended up blaming himself for it. "The doctor's said that there was a high chance that you wouldn't make it," he said. "I got so desperate that I did whatever I could to keep you warm. After that, I just prayed for a sign that you would make it." He takes my hand and says, "And here you are. I'm so, so sorry."

A part of me couldn't believe any word he said, but it was *how* he said it that made me think otherwise. He sounded remorseful and guilty and as if he were in pain. Maybe he was hurting. For whatever reason I don't know. He seemed lost at first, and now he's had a sense of clarity.

What I'd been hoping for him to see had finally happened. He finally saw through me and saw that nothing was different about me. That I was exactly who I was before I came out to him. He sees it now, and he wants to make things right. He's changed, maybe not all at once, but something has changed.

But still…

"You hunted me down," I say. "You chased me like a dog and tried to send me away."

"I know," he says, "and I'm sorry." He repeats it over and over again. "I'm so, so sorry."

I want to forgive him, I really do. But a part of me is still hurting. A lot has happened between us, from the beatings to the harassment. Still, something inside of him changed, and he wants to make things right. I guess I'll forgive him some day.

I just need time.

Still, he waits for an answer. He's still holding my hand, so I hold it back. My dad looks down and then to me. His lips curve into a smile. I don't smile back. He leans forward and gives me a hug. "I love you," he says.

Despite still holding some pain in me, I wrap my arms around him and hug him back.

28

Four weeks later.

The Sunday sermon comes to an end with Marcus wishing everyone a good day. Marcus walks out of the church and then the families go after him. The same thing will happen as always. Marcus will be standing outside, saying goodbye to passing parents, shaking hands and offering any advice. Some parents will stay around talking to one another. Once everyone's gone, Marcus will get to work in planning for the next sermon.

I'm still not a fan of Sunday sermons, but today's sermon was different from the others. Matthew's father talked about the importance of loving one another with the help of a few scriptures and sayings that helped him out. He also brought in topics that his predecessor didn't bring up at all. Parents nodded along with it. I did as well, but I knew better. He didn't just plan this up in one week. He'd been planning this since Matthew and I came back, since he and my dad had a change of heart.

It came to Matthew as a surprise, but it was the truth. When he got back, both his mom and dad hugged him, kissed him, and told him how much they loved him. He told me how they promised to change, and from what Matthew's been saying, they really are trying. "They still have a long way to go," Matthew said. "But I can see they're doing their best." I've seen it too. They invited my family to dinner, and they seemed "comfortable" with us being together.

They still have a long way to go, but they're really trying.

The same thing is going for my dad. Since I was discharged from the hospital and came home, he's never done anything to say that he's still angry. In fact, he's becoming more open about my identity. He's been doing research, asking me about it, and giving me support. He's still uncomfortable about the whole thing, especially when he sees me with Matthew, but he's still trying, and that's what matters.

I asked my mom about the sudden change in him. "Have you forgiven him?" I ask.

"A bit," she said. "Wounds heal with time, and at least he's trying to be better."

That's all the assurance I need. Since we got back, the topic of the divorce hasn't come up, and so far, all seems to be going well. There are no more arguments, pep talks, or plans for conversion therapy. My dad cancelled all the paperwork and called it off. For once since I came out, I feel like I don't have to look over my shoulder.

I move out of my seat and head towards the door. My parents stay behind talking to a family of four that recently moved here. I met them over dinner, and they seemed nice. They don't strike me as the super conservative types, so whenever they find out that I have a boyfriend, they probably won't make such a huge issue of it. Now that I think of it, most parents have been supporting me and Matthew since we got back. The rest are against it, doing anything to show it by judging us when they see us doing anything, including talking behind our backs. Some are still coming around, and I do my best when they try to act normal around me.

Overall, I can say that things are looking up for us.

Our parents are supporting us, the town is getting used to us, and our lives are going back to normal, or as normal as they can go back to. Things don't ever go back to normal after sharing news like this, but at least we can adapt to it, and we have.

Eventually, I come across Mr. and Mrs. Bartow who as usual, look at me distastefully as I go by. I ignore their stares. I know they are about more than my sexuality. I told them about how I saw Kyle when I got back to town. They said some things, but I took a stand and told them how they failed as parents for what they've done to him, and I haven't said a word to them since, not even when he called me two weeks ago.

To be honest, I was surprised when I found out it was him. I never actually expected to see or hear from him again. The call was very quick, and he only told me that he was safe and sound up north. He didn't tell me where he was and probably never will. He did say that he'll come back someday, but the day may vary. "Maybe when I'm eighteen or something," he said. "I'll come back and show my parents that I'm more than just who I date."

That was the last thing he said to me, and from there, I haven't heard anything else. I can only hope that whatever path he goes through in life is the one he thinks is best for him.

When I get to the door, most of the families had made their way to it, creating a literal sea of moving bodies trying to make their way out through the same small door. It'll take some time, but I can wait. I'm not in a rush to leave. I'm hoping to talk to Matthew before I go. By now, he must be outside with his dad. I try to peek through the sea of moving bodies in search of him, but so far, he's nowhere to be found. I'll see him after the crowd moves by.

At that moment, I feel a hand touch my shoulder and I turn around. I smile. "Hey," I say to Matthew.

"Hey," he says back. "Were you looking for me?"

I nod. "I wanted to tell you something."

"Me too, but you go first."

"I was wondering if maybe you want to hang out. My parents have some things to do so I have the rest of the day to kill. You free?"

Matthew nods. "Sure thing. Do you wanna invite Nora and Alex?"

I shake my head. "They're actually busy. Alex is taking her out to a festival in the next town over."

"Really?"

"Yeah, really. Alex and Nora thought it was time and Nora looked excited when she told me about it."

Matthew smiles. "Hard to believe they're finally gonna start dating."

I raise my shoulders. "Well, I've been waiting for this to happen longer than you, so I'm actually glad that they're doing it."

"You think it'll go well?"

"We can only hope."

"Yeah, we can." A few seconds of silence. "So, what do you have in mind for us to do?"

I snicker. "I actually don't have a plan, but we can figure something out. Maybe we could just walk around town, hold hands, talk, maybe share a kiss."

Matthew smiles and I smile back. It's nice to know that after everything that happened, we don't have to hide anymore. We can kiss in the middle of town and not be worried that we'll be ratted to our parents. The only problem we'll face is the bigots that have an issue with it, but they'll never bring us down. They'll only win if we let them, and so far, they haven't been able to bring us down, not even once.

"I have something to show you," Matthew says. "Give me a minute."

Matthew walks back towards his mom where he talks to her for a bit before coming back with something in his hands. It's the brown leather journal I bought for him back in the city, but it looked different. It still had the same brown leather exterior, but there was something new about it, something unique. Maybe it was the way Matthew looked. It was almost as if it held more sentimental value than it already had.

Matthew extends the journal to me. "I want you to have it," he says.

I take it in my hands. "But it's yours," I say. "Whatever you wrote in it is only for you."

"Well, what I wrote in it was for the two of us." He takes my hand. "Inside it, you'll find our story, or as much as I could put in detail. I may not have put all that's happened, but the most important pieces are there. I felt like preserving our story, and this is my way of doing so." Matthew snaps his fingers. "There's one more thing."

Matthew pulls out his phone and then shows me a picture. It's a photo of us in his bedroom, a selfie we took with his camera. It's black and white with different tones of light and darkness blending in. Matthew's face is buried into my cheek as he kisses me. I'm smiling as I have my arm stretched out as I took the picture. I smile. "Wow," I say.

"I know," he replies putting his phone back in his pocket. "I've got a couple of other pictures printed out in the car. You can have some if you want."

Photos of us and our story written in paper. My mind is blown away.

Still… "Are you sure it's safe to have those around," I ask. "What about our parents?"

"Don't worry about it. They're changing and this is just going to show them how much we love each other. The hard part is over. We don't need to be afraid of what our parents will do anymore. Now we can just be who we are."

I look down at the journal and run a hand over its cover. I open it up and stare at the first page. *A Love Story* was written in the center, in his handwriting. I smile. It looks so beautiful. I flip the page and stare at the writing. "I'm afraid I can't read your handwriting," I say.

Matthew laughs. "Then I guess that means that I'll have to read it to you, if you want."

I smile and plant my lips on his. A few onlookers pass us by and watch us. Some smile, others look disgusted. The latter doesn't bother me anymore. I no longer care what they think. Their hate is no excuse for me to feeling bad. I find strength in that.

I pull away from Matthew and stare into his eyes. They sparkle even more than they did before. My smile widens. Matthew smiles back and leans into my ear. "I love you," he says.

I smile. "I love you too."

I find it hard to believe that not that long ago, my life was in tatters. My dad hated me, my mom was unsure, and I felt lonelier than ever before. Then I met Matthew, and he took my heart and gave me a joy that no one else ever has. Through him, I found strength and with him, I'd go to the edge of all things. We met hard times, and it seemed that fate was against us. But it all worked out in the end. We're back here, where it all began, out in the open and free, and there's nothing better than that.

"Shall we go?" Matthew asks.

"We shall," I say.

I take Matthew's hand in mine and squeeze it gently. And from there, we walk into the world.

The End.

About the Author

Enrique Muchacho grew up in Puerto Rico. He began writing when he was 16, not long after becoming an avid reader. Muchacho likes to tell stories, and looks to find new ways of doing so in whatever way possible. He is currently studying at Loyola University Maryland, hoping to graduate with a degree in writing and journalism. *A Love Story* is his first novel.

Apprentice
House Press
Loyola University Maryland

Apprentice House is the country's only campus-based, student-staffed book
publishing company. Directed by professors and industry professionals, it is
a nonprofit activity of the Communication Department at Loyola University
Maryland.

Using state-of-the-art technology and an experiential learning model of
education, Apprentice House publishes books in untraditional ways. This
dual responsibility as publishers and educators creates an unprecedented
collaborative environment among faculty and students, while teaching
tomorrow's editors, designers, and marketers.

Outside of class, progress on book projects is carried forth by the AH Book
Publishing Club, a co-curricular campus organization supported by Loyola
University Maryland's Office of Student Activities.

Eclectic and provocative, Apprentice House titles intend to entertain as well
as spark dialogue on a variety of topics. Financial contributions to sustain
the press's work are welcomed. Contributions are tax deductible to the fullest
extent allowed by the IRS.

To learn more about Apprentice House books or to obtain submission
guidelines, please visit www.apprenticehouse.com.

Apprentice House
Communication Department
Loyola University Maryland
4501 N. Charles Street
Baltimore, MD 21210
410-617-5265 • info@apprenticehouse.com • www.apprenticehouse.com